BREATHLESS

MERCILESS SERIES BOOK 3

W WINTERS

AUTHOR'S COPYRIGHT

ABOUT

Breathless
Book 3

Her lips tasted like Cabernet and her touch was like fire.

I was blinded by what she did to me. I so easily fell for something I thought I'd never have.

I was weak for her and should have known better. I should have known she could never love a man like me.

She brought out a side of me that I wish had stayed dead.

I won't make the same mistake twice.

I don't care how much she begs me.

I don't care that I crave her more than anything else...

This is book 3 in the Merciless series. It picks up right where book 2, *Heartless*, left off. They must be read in order.

Dedicated to Bethany.

Thank you for reading my cards.
And everything that came with it.
xoxo

A special thanks to my editing team and betas who make my
books what they are.
Donna, Chris, Becca, Teresa, Katie, TJ, and Sophie – I
couldn't do this without you.
#TeamWillow

CHAPTER 1

Carter

IT'S BEEN a long time since someone has dared try to kill me in my own home.

Even longer since someone has pointed a gun at me and lived to tell the tale.

I can barely hear a damn thing due to the ringing in my ears. I've waited for this moment, but this isn't how I thought it would go.

She loves me, I remind myself. She fucking loves me. I know she does.

Aria's face is flushed, and her hand trembles as she fights to hold the gun steady.

I take one step toward her and she cocks it. The click fills the room. Whatever remaining semblance of a heart I had shatters in my chest, the small shards shooting waves of pain through my body.

The sick grin on my face wanes even as I struggle to hold it in place, focusing on those gorgeous hazel eyes. Eyes that drew me to her, that begged me for mercy, that made me feel more than I've felt in years.

Eyes that fooled me.

"Drop your guns," Aria demands, her voice shaky but clear and loud regardless. It's fucking insane that in this moment she strikes me as utterly gorgeous. In her strength, she's at her most beautiful.

"Drop them!" she calls out more strongly and the gun wavers. It's obvious she's never held one before, or at the very least, never fired one.

Yet, she's pointing it at me. It could go off accidentally, killing me. *Would she regret it?* I question and feel a strong tug in my chest. A well of emotion threatens to break my composure. Every inch of skin is numb as I stare at the barrel, feeling everything crumble around me.

In front of the enemy.

In front of my brothers.

In front of her.

"Carter?" I hear Jase without seeing him, asking if they're to listen to her or not.

Two of my brothers, Jase and Declan, are behind me with guns pointed at three men kneeling on the floor. Two of them are her cousins, and the third man is her former lover and friend. The name she prayed to while in the cell, the one name I'm tired of hearing her speak, belongs to him.

All three are men who wanted to kill us only moments ago. Men that Aria is protecting, and willing to kill me to save.

Those fucking shards dig deeper into whatever wound they've gouged in my chest.

Swallowing the knot in my throat along with the distress I'm feeling, I answer Jase although I don't take my gaze from Aria. "Drop them." Instantly, relief shows on Aria's face, and she even relaxes her grip on the gun until I add, "But don't let those fuckers have them. No one holds a gun," I swallow thickly and add, forcing a smirk to my face, "but Aria."

The control is still in my demand. They'll listen to me, everyone who's worth a damn in this room will... but as time passes, I can feel it slipping away. I can only imagine what her family thinks, but it's what my brothers are seeing that fucking shreds me. They know I love her.

And now they're watching her betray all of us.

"Let them go," Aria commands in a weaker tone, one filled with a plea. Visibly swallowing, she finally breaks my gaze to look at them. Her startled, sharp intake of breath at what she sees destroys me. Her mercy and compassion for them are sickening.

They came to kill me. She fucking knows that.

She might kill me yet.

I loved her. I know I loved her, and that was my first mistake.

Anger rises and rings in my blood. My sanity finally comes back to me, hardening me and reminding me of who I am and everything I've worked for.

It's all going to crumble. All because of her.

I would have done *anything* for her.

"Let's go." I hear Nikolai's voice, low and riddled with pain. The blood is still bright red from the split on his lip and a bruise has already formed on his face. My knuckles turn white as my fist tightens. All I need is one moment to take out every bit of my aggression on him. I want to break his jaw for daring to speak those words to my Aria.

I've never felt rage like I do now as he reaches for her like he can take her away from me.

Because he can.

Because she's willing.

"Go," she says, and Aria's voice is strong as she glances at him. Again, the gun is slack in her grip. She doesn't seem to notice how loose the gun is in her hands. I could take it; I could chance it. But it would risk putting her in danger, and my gaze falls at the thought.

"Now," one of her cousins hiss, tugging on Nikolai's arm. The shirt tightens around his neck as the fabric is pulled. Peeking at him from my periphery, I'm disgusted, as is Nikolai, judging by his expression.

"Come with us," Nikolai urges, raising his voice to command her, but also beg her, and I take my focus from Aria, staring at the man Nikolai is.

He reminds me of the boy I once was.

Foolish and reckless. But he never went through the shit I did. He was bred into this life, he wasn't thrown into it and forced to fight to survive every fucking day.

Yet he thinks he can take her.

"I'm staying," Aria says with authority before I can say anything. Her declaration makes Nikolai flinch. A small bit of hope flutters in my chest. My throat tightens, and my chest aches, feeling as if it's on the verge of ripping wide open. *She's staying.*

"We don't have time for this!" one of her cousins yells out, glancing around the room as if any minute now, I'll change my mind and kill them all.

He'd be right if it wasn't for Aria.

She wanted them. She chose them.

"I'm not leaving without you," Nikolai growls and stalks to Aria, ready to take her. That's my cue to reach for my gun.

Their reunion has lasted long enough, and I refuse to let him take her. No one will take her from me. No one.

Adrenaline races through my blood, my breathing coming in heavier as my jaw clenches. The gun is hot in my hand. Hotter than it's ever felt before. It's pointed at Nikolai; Aria's is pointed at me.

My voice is deep and rough as I tell the three of them, "You have two minutes to run."

"Carter," she says, and Aria's voice is a desperate plea, but she has no room to bargain and I have no mercy remaining, not even for her. I ignore her, feeling the rage from what she's done seep into the marrow of my bones as I finish stating, "and then we'll open fire."

My brothers move slowly, reaching for their guns as Aria's expression crumples with pain and she rocks backward toward the wall, with her nervousness evident.

Nikolai's jaw is tense, his light blue eyes sparking with hate. "Come with me," he says beneath his breath. "Take her!" he commands his allies.

But they run, leaving him alone and leaving her behind. "She had her chance!" one of the men yells behind him. Their sneakers squeak as their footsteps pound on the freshly polished floor. Cowards. Talvery men are cowards.

"Aria, please," Nikolai begs her as if it breaks his fucking heart. Fuck him.

"One minute," I grit between my teeth and he finally looks at me. My grip tightens on the gun. One squeeze of the trigger and I'd be rid of him forever. I'm so close to pulling it, just to end it all. He looks me in the eyes and I wish the look I give him back was enough to kill him.

"Go," she whimpers, her eyes flickering from my gun to him. "Get out of here!" she screams at him.

"I'll come back for you," he tells her as if she's his long-lost love.

I hope he does come back for her. My nostrils flare and my chest aches as she gasps for breath watching him leave. *Come back for her, Nikolai. Come back, so I can break your fucking neck.* I bite my tongue, tasting the metallic tang of blood in my mouth.

I will kill him if it's the last thing I do.

He's still running away from her. My blunt nails dig into my palms as my fists tighten and the anger and jealousy mix into a deadly concoction. Red bleeds into my vision and it's all I can do not to pull the trigger as it follows his movements.

"I wanted to tell you," Aria sobs as the sound of Nikolai running away fades in the hallway. "I didn't think--"

"Tell me what?" I ask her.

"That they were coming," she says with a pain in her voice that matches the one swirling in her eyes. She's breaking apart, barely breathing and I can see the regret, the remorse. But only one thing resonates with me.

"You knew?" I question her and feel a chill rush through my body that sinks all the way to my bones.

She never loved me. She never did. You protect the ones you love. Always. And she didn't protect me.

I was a fucking fool and she isn't the woman I thought she is. She's a fucking liar.

"Are we really letting them go?" Declan's question slices through the haze of disbelief and treachery.

"You knew?" I ask her again, my temper coming back anew.

"I, I..." she stutters over her words, her gaze darting over my face, fear and pain causing her hazel eyes to glass over with tears. She lowers her gun all the way

7

down, not daring to point it at me anymore and I drop mine as I move closer to her, each heavy step sounding more foreboding than the last.

"Carter?" Declan yells my name, demanding an answer.

With each step closer to her, she takes one in reverse until her shoulders hit the wall.

I holster my gun before ripping hers out of her hands, although she doesn't put up a fight. "Carter," Declan calls out again, not caring at all that the woman I loved set me up. She knew they were coming to kill me, to kill all of us, and she did *nothing*. "Are we letting them go or not?" Declan asks.

With one hand braced on the wall above Aria's head and the other pinning her hip to it, I look her dead in the eyes, ignoring everything about her gaze that draws me in. She can't have that anymore. I'm taking that power away.

Feeling the dominance of hatred flow through me and wanting to hurt her as she's hurt me, I answer Declan in a deep voice that's barely audible. "Kill them all."

* * *

Jase

I'M quick to follow Declan out of the room, even

though I know it's a mistake to leave Carter alone with Aria.

I'll be fast. I have to do something to stop this.

"Declan." Raising my voice, I call out to my brother and the sound of his footsteps echoing in the hallway stops instantly. He turns to me, anger and tension still rolling off of his shoulders.

He can barely look me in the eyes.

"Yeah?" His voice is tight as I make my way to him, closing the distance as quickly as I can.

I keep my voice as low as possible and ignore the banging of my heart against my ribcage as I look over my shoulder to make sure no one followed, to make sure no one can hear me defy my brother's orders.

"Don't tell them to shoot to kill." I start to talk before I've even fully faced him. My words are mixed with my tense breath from the adrenaline flowing through my blood. "If they shoot, tell them to make sure they miss."

Declan hears me; I know he does by the shock on his face. The roar of anger coming from the foyer behind me reminds me of how unhinged Carter has become. He's going to do something stupid. Something he'll never be able to take back.

"I'm going back to them," I tell Declan and turn away only to have him grip my arm and pull me back to him. He doesn't say anything at first, but I can see the question in his eyes, the feel of betrayal from him.

And it shreds me.

"You know he loves her," I tell him, feeling the ache

of sadness rising inside me. It hurt Carter, but it's more than that. She betrayed us all.

"Not after that," Declan nearly whispers. Shaking his head slightly with a defeated expression on his face, he continues, "Not after she--"

"It's not her fault she had to choose," I push the words through my clenched teeth, knowing in my gut that she's fighting with what's right versus where her loyalties should lie. "She never should have known."

The tension in Declan's gaze wavers, and he looks behind me before reaching my eyes again.

"She made a choice to stay. Let Talvery know that. She chose to stay. It'll fucking kill Nikolai and make the crack in their factions that much deeper. Nikolai has to live."

I know Carter will be pissed at me, but he'll get over it. He'll thank me when it's all said and done. It has to go down like this. I can't let him ruin everything.

With a tight nod, Declan runs his thumb over his chin but doesn't say a word.

"Tell the guards to let them go back to Talvery. But make sure they all know she chose to stay. She chose Carter."

CHAPTER 2

Aria

I'VE ALWAYS KNOWN Carter to be a beast of a man. Barely contained and waiting for an outlet to release his rage. As his chest rises and falls with each heavy intake of breath and his muscles coil, his shoulders get more and more tense. With each ragged second of anxiousness passing between us, I know there's nothing holding him back.

"You chose them." His words are calculated, spoken with control although he looks anything but in control. The tension winds tighter and my body grows hotter with every hard thud in my chest.

"No," I try to tell him although my throat constricts to the point where I think I can't breathe. I start to shake my head, but he lets out a snarl, flipping the front table over in one swift movement. The carved wood antique crashes into the wall with a loud bang that forces my body to tremble as he screams, "Get out!"

The rough cadence of his voice carries through the room and I back away from him, my shoulders hunching as fear consumes me.

Tears prick my eyes and I try to speak, to tell him I didn't have a choice. I just did what I thought I needed to. "I'd never have--"

He turns to me, taking three large strides forward, the cords in his neck taut and bulging as his dark eyes pierce into me.

"Shot me?" he questions me with nothing but disbelief and rage burning in his eyes.

The intensity of his stare alone makes me cower.

"Carter," Jase speaks up from behind us, but Carter doesn't turn away from me. He stares at me like I've betrayed him. As if what I did was the ultimate sin.

Has he forgotten that they're my family? That I've begged him to spare them and yet he was going to execute them? Did he forget that he stole me from them and locked me in a cell for weeks?

He stares down at me as though he hates me.

I feel it. It's raw and palpable.

At this moment, I feel he truly hates me. And that's what breaks me.

Because no matter what he did to me, I never hated him. *I love him.*

Tears flow from me easily as Carter informs Jase in

the most unfeeling manner that I'm to be removed from the premises.

My heart hollows and collapses, but my feet move, my body shoves me forward. And Carter follows, blocking me from running down the hall to the bedroom.

"I thought you loved me," he sneers at me and I cover my mouth with my hand to hold back the agony.

I do love him. I do.

I swear I love this man.

Even if he hurt me and even if I hurt him just now.

I can't voice a single word as his warm breath covers my face and my body wracks with a sob.

"Carter!" Jase yells, grabbing his shoulder and forcing him to look at anything other than me.

The moment he does, I bolt. I turn to run past Jase. I don't dare try to run past Carter. He could block me, catch me, and throw me away. He could see to it himself to banish me from his home.

The hideaway room is past the bedroom, so that space isn't an option either. And given the state Carter's in, I don't trust him to keep his word and let me recover from what's happened, so I can try to explain.

Instead, I run as fast as I can, on shaky legs and with adrenaline coursing through me, in the opposite direction. The muscles in my thighs scream with pain as I take the stairs two at a time. The pounding of my heart and footsteps are overwhelming. I'm hot and sweating and not okay in any sense of the word. I have to make him understand somehow.

He starts chasing me, although at his own slow and teasing pace. The second I hear Carter behind me, I slip. My elbow and hand crash on the hard, wooden stairs as does my knee, sending shooting pains through my body. I could cry, and I hate myself for it. I did this. This is my fault. I look behind me and see Carter start to climb the stairs. A mask of anger and dominance appears set in stone on his handsome features.

The cell.

The thought hits me at that moment. I force myself to get up and run to the cell. I know it's behind a painting. He wouldn't be able to get in if I ran to the cell and locked myself in. It'll take him time to get a key; time I desperately need. He needs to calm down and I need time. Time so I can figure out how to explain things to him in a way he'll understand.

Running up the stairs and using that momentum to push off the wall at the top, I careen down the hall.

Which one is it? My breathing is unsteady and a cold sweat breaks out along every inch of my skin. My heart won't stop racing; pounding chaotically. I can barely see straight.

There are six large paintings in the hall and my fingers fumble around the first, trying to heave it to the side, but it's not the right one. I tremble as my gaze is whipped toward the sound of him coming.

The second painting I push so hard that it falls, nearly toppling over on me. It's at least five feet long and four feet high. And it's not the right one either. The frame splits and cracks and I have to high-step over it, scraping my shin as I go, but I don't care. *Where is it? I need to find it, please.*

"You can't run from me." Carter's deep voice reverberates through the hall, and glancing behind me, I see his shadow as he climbs the stairs.

Thump, thump, my heart pounds harder and harder. I can barely breathe.

I don't know which one is the cell. I don't know.

The box.

The very thought has me sprinting down the hall to the last set of stairs. Up one more floor and on the left. I run as fast as I can, gasping for breath. Just the idea of Carter not giving me a chance to even speak to him, to explain, to ask for forgiveness, is crushing me with every step.

He just needs time. He has to understand. I can make him understand.

Visions of his face when I pointed the gun at him flash through my mind as I run.

Carter, seemingly over the desire to move slowly and let me run from him, picks up his pace as I get to the hall. I can hear his footsteps pound up the stairs, so I run as hard as I can, nearly slamming into the closed door of his office. Tears prick as the hurt and betrayal of what I've done set in.

I scrabble with the knob so clumsily in my own chaos that I think it's locked, but it's not.

It's open and a wave of relief runs through me

although it's short-lived. Nothing is okay at this moment. Not a damn thing is all right.

I don't waste any time; I don't bother to close the office door either. Sprinting to the box, I rip the top open and practically fall into it, scraping my thighs and back. A scream is ripped from me, but it's merely instinctual. I don't care about the pain; I don't care about anything other than shutting the lid and locking myself in.

I have to reach up to get the top of it lowered and when I do, I see Carter in the doorway. Fear paralyzes me when I see his face, contorted with a look of outrage and red from running. My skin is ice cold as I reach for the lid. My fingertips feel numb as I slam it down.

There's a snap, I hear it, but I don't know what it is. It comes with a tug at the back of my neck that's accompanied by a sharp pinch I try to ignore as my fingers slip along the edge of the lid searching for the lock.

Shrouded in darkness, I struggle to find the lock, hearing Carter's footsteps getting closer and closer, but my trembling fingers find it and the multiple clicks assure me I'm bolted in.

All I can hear is my staggered breathing for a moment and then another.

With a deafening roar of anger, the box lifts off the ground only an inch, if that. Through my tears still streaking down my hot face, I can see Carter lifting it with all his strength, but it's meant to outlast such acts and so it does.

Crouched in the box and gripping on to myself, I hold my breath knowing he can't do a damn thing about it.

It's only then that I hear the rolling of the beads. It's only then that I feel the pearls rolling around me. I shriek in terror at first, thinking that something is alive and in the dark place with me. But it's only my necklace. The beads that have fallen off the broken chain.

Tears leak freely at the realization.

My chest hollows as I cover my mouth to keep from crying harder.

The box moves a little more and I close my eyes until he drops it, making my body sway and tumble in the small amount of space I have. A small yelp escapes me, but I focus on calming down. I'm on the verge of a panic attack or worse.

My eyes are closed tighter than they've ever been. Shock and horror still threaten to suffocate me as I struggle to inhale.

A few minutes pass and all I can hear is Carter's chaotic breathing. For a moment someone comes in, I think Jase, speaking quietly and trying to tell Carter to calm down, but the door closes shut with a loud click and then there's silence again.

Nothing but silence and the slamming of my own heartbeat and the rushing of blood in my ears.

It's going to be okay, I try to reassure myself. *He has to understand.* Even the thought is fleeting in my mind. All

Carter knows is that I chose them, my family and his enemies. I pointed a gun at him and cocked it.

Oh, my God. My head spins as the memory comes back to me.

I threatened the life of the only man I've ever loved.

When I finally open my eyes, Carter's are fixed directly on mine. As if he can see me, even though I know it's impossible. His dark eyes pierce through me, pinning me where I am and eliciting a new kind of fear.

His deep voice sends a jagged spike of despair through me as he says low beneath his breath, "You can't stay in there forever."

CHAPTER 3

Carter

I'VE NEVER in my life felt like this before.

The clock ticks as time passes. I can count on one hand every time I've been betrayed, but it's never felt like this because none of them were close to me. I've never let anyone in.

Not the guards I've depended on, not the boys I took in to help. I didn't feel betrayed by them when they only stole from me or tried to bargain with someone else who wanted me dead.

I've never let a soul close to me other than my brothers. So, no one can hurt me.

No outsider has ever been close to me... except for her, the only woman I ever loved.

A chill rolls through my body like the unrelenting

tides of the ocean. The adrenaline has waned as I sit here in the chair, staring at that fucking box. My knuckles are bruised and cut, but I keep putting pressure on them, to keep me from thinking of a different pain, the aching in my chest.

Every time I blink, the barrel of her gun is there, staring back at me.

"Carter." Daniel's voice breaks me from my thoughts and brings me back to this reality. It fucking hurts; every piece of me hurts. Sitting up slightly in the chair, I finally take my eyes away from the box, away from Aria. I tilt my head as I take in my brother and the man standing next to him. Eli's one of our guards and head of security.

"Eli's finished the walk-through." He's struggling to keep his eyes on me; I can see it in the way he swallows visibly and clenches his hands. Even his voice is strained.

She did this. I know Daniel cared about her. And she betrayed him like she did me.

Eli steps forward to speak, telling me about each of the bombs they found and disposed of and where exactly the Talvery men ran. No surprises and nothing I give a fuck about at this point. Not when the woman who caused all of this is still right in front of me, but safely hiding in plain sight.

"All of them?" I ask just to pretend to be present, pressing my sore back into the chair and still staring at the fucking box. I can barely see Eli nod in my periphery as he answers, "Yes, sir." With his shoulders squared and his hands behind his back, he looks like the soldier he used to be.

But he defied me.

"You let them live," I say flatly, turning my attention directly to him for just a second, so he can see how pissed I am, hardening my gaze and my scowl. Then I look back to the box. The box I took from a man I refused to show mercy to. Aria's breathing picks up and she moves within its small confinements.

"I ordered Eli and the guards to let them live." Jase's voice sends a cold trickle down my neck. It's hard to swallow as my blood heats with anger.

One by one, they're all turning their backs on me.

Aria moves inside of the box again; I can faintly hear her crying. It's then that Eli catches on to the fact that she's in the box. Glancing at him, I can see his expression fall, the puzzle in his head forming as each of the pieces fall into place.

It takes a moment for him to fix his fucking face and wipe the look of disgust off of it.

She did this. She will suffer the consequences.

I gave her a chance; I would have given her anything had she simply chosen me. I was stupid for ever loving her. Or for thinking she loved me.

"Leave," I bite out the command, feeling the raw word scratch against the back of my throat. Eli's the first to turn around sharply and leave at once. Daniel and Jase step forward rather than retreating and my muscles tense, my teeth gritting as I lean forward in the seat I haven't left for nearly an hour now.

"Carter," my brother says, and Jase's voice is strong and demanding. Not like the way Aria's been saying it as she whimpers in the box, begging me to understand. I won't hear it. There's no excuse.

"Fuck off." It's all I can say back to him. The rage blisters inside of me, eating me alive that they all defied me.

"Carter." Daniel's tone is softer, more placating. "Just relax for a minute. Calm down," he tells me.

I can barely inhale, refusing to believe everything that's happened.

"Did you hear that, songbird?" I ask her rather than facing my brothers. The legs of the chair scratch against the floor as I lean forward, searching for a seam in the box where I think she can see me. I stare at it with an unforgiving bitterness as I tell her, "I just need to calm down."

I can feel the depth of emotion roaring inside of me as Jase speaks, "It was an unfortunate event, but we can use this to our favor."

"Unfortunate?" I can't hide the disbelief and venom in my voice as I stare back at him, finally rising from my seat. The force of the abrupt movement shoves the chair back. All I can hear is my heart beat in time with my heavy footsteps as I move closer to my brother.

Same height as me, the same determination in his voice.

"Knock it off," Daniel says and walks between us, separating us with a hard hand on both of our chests. "What about Aria?" he says quickly as he pushes me back. His glare pleads with me to think about something other than her apparent betrayal. "She's not okay." He lowers his voice to tell me the obvious and then lets his gaze move to her before looking back at me.

"What about her?" I ask him in a hardened tone. My hands form fists so tightly, I can feel the skin across my knuckles nearly crack and the cuts that are there split even wider.

A whimper from the box catches the attention of my brothers, both of them looking toward her as I stare at them.

"What the fuck do you even care for?" I sneer at Daniel. I raise my voice to remind them of the hard truth, "She chose them."

The sobs return from the box behind me and it enrages me. "Now she cries," I say, talking to her more than to them as I walk closer to where she is. The box is off-center now, crooked and making the end of the rug uneven from my useless attempts to open it even though I know it can't be done.

"She wasn't crying when she held a gun to my head!" Everything turns to white noise. Whatever my brothers say, the relentless crying from the woman I loved as she hides from me for fear of her own life, all of it.

I hate everything at this moment. I hate everyone. But I hate myself the most.

"She wasn't crying when she found out her family was coming to kill us. To kill all of us!" The last bit comes out louder and harsher than I can control, and I reach above the box to the bookshelves, shoving aside a row of them. The hardcovers and pages fly into a flutter before slamming down on the floor.

"I was!" Again, I hear her cry out, "I was!"

But all it does is fuel me to continue wrecking every shelf above her. All of the books falling around her, some of them slamming against the box, only make her cry out louder.

I hate her.

I hate them all.

I hate everything.

It takes both of my brothers to pull me back against the office window and away from the shelves. As I catch my breath, I think about destroying all of it. Wrecking every piece of this rich interior. It mocks me. It's a façade of control and I have none anymore. Not a damn shred of control.

"You never loved me!" I scream at her. "I should have kept you in that fucking cell until you knew better than to defy me!"

"Please, Carter, let me explain," she weeps.

"I was too fucking good to you," I sneer at her as loud as I can, feeling my composure deteriorate just as any ounce of mercy has. I scream at the top of my lungs, wanting to shred something apart. Every last bit of my humanity will do.

"Stop," Daniel says, his head close to mine. As he uses all of his strength to push me against the cold glass window, he's so close that I can feel the burn of his body heat.

"It's okay," he tells me as Jase grunts, his expression strained and his face red with exertion. Every inch of my skin is numb with a pain I've never felt before.

I want to tell them all nothing is okay and that I'll never stop. Never. There's nothing left of me but this shell of a man. But before I can tell them that I'll find the men they let get away and I'll rip out their fucking throats before they can breathe a word of how Aria betrayed me, a small voice comes from the doorway.

"Fuck." Daniel barely breathes the word before releasing me to run to her, to Addison, but he's too late.

I don't know how much Addison saw, or what she saw, but her face is pale.

Aria's still crying uncontrollably, and it's going to be obvious. It's obvious I'm hurting her and that she's scared. She's scared of me because I've fucking lost it. Nothing else matters.

There's no hiding now. Not from my brothers, not from the Talverys. Not from Addison, the one connection I still have to my brother Tyler.

Shame and disgust are a painful cocktail to swallow, but I choke it down.

"What the fuck are you doing?" Addison's voice vacillates between strength and panic as she stands in the doorway to my office. Her eyes dart from me to Daniel.

"How long have you been standing there?" Daniel asks Addison.

"Long enough... to..." Addison struggles to even look at Daniel. "You're hurting her," Addison barely glances my way.

Aria's sobs are punctuated with hiccups as she breathes in heavily, like she's desperate to stop, desperate to quiet her cries.

"Aria?" Addison's tone reflects a despair I've never heard from her before and inside I shatter. Whatever bit of anger that lingered, fragments and scatters in the pit of my stomach. Sucking in a deep, shuddering breath, her eyes go wide with fear and she takes a half step back.

"Daniel," she says hesitantly, her eyes wide with shame and disbelief as her body shakes so strongly I can see it from across the room. "You can't be okay with this?"

Fuck. Fuck. It's all fucked!

I straighten my stance as Jase lets go of me, moving out of the way and taking a few strides closer to Aria, away from me and out of sight from Addison. But the movement makes him that much more obvious to her.

"Get her out," she says, and her demand is strained by the veil of fear. She's pointing to the box but doesn't dare to let it steal her gaze from Daniel.

"Addison, stay out of it," Daniel tells her as he takes another step closer to her, his hands held in the air.

"Are you fucking serious?" As each word cracks with disdain, pain grows on her face. "Daniel, help her." The last word comes out in a croak as she backs away from him, further into the office and closer to the shelves. She nearly trips on the fallen books but manages to keep herself upright. She only takes her eyes off of him to see where Jase and I are. Neither of us is moving as she struggles to get closer to the box, closer to Aria who's quiet, and for a moment, I worry if she's all right.

"Why did he say cell?" Addison asks, and I can't even begin to think of when I said that word or how I used it. All I can see is red and my memory is a white fog.

"Addison, please," Daniel begs her.

"He's hurting her, putting her in a cell?" she shrieks and then turns any bit of remorse or disgust into anger. "You're allowing it! You knew!"

"She put herself in there," I say, cutting off the interrogation directed at Daniel and feeling the need to defend us against Addison's unspoken, yet all too clear thoughts. "Tell her, Aria." I raise my voice, feeling my cold blood fill my veins and praying to hear her voice.

"What did you do to her?" Addison's breathy words are filled with accusations.

"Nothing." Aria's voice is finally heard, although it trembles and is minuscule compared to ours.

With a hardened jaw, I dare to stare back at her, narrowing my gaze and not allowing her to blame this on me.

"She ran up here and hid because she held a gun to my head." Each word comes out harder, but I stay where I am as Addison inches closer to Aria.

"Addison," Daniel says as he tries to reason with her, keeping his voice low, but not to be denied, "get out."

"Fuck you," she spits at him and then finally lays a hand on the box.

"Aria," she calls out to her, banging the palm of her hand on the box behind her, although she still faces Daniel with a defiant expression on her face.

Aria whimpers for Addison to go, to leave her alone and stay out of it.

"I'm not going anywhere," Addison's quick to reply, tears leaking down her face.

"Don't cry," Daniel pleads with her, stepping forward and trying to reach out for Addison. The resulting slap is so hard, so vicious, I practically feel it against my own skin. Daniel's cheek instantly turns bright red, his head rotating back slowly to face her as Addison screeches at him, "Don't touch me!"

"Addison, you need to." Daniel barely gets another word out before Addison loses her shit entirely. Her voice three octaves higher than it should be, her entire body shaking with a new kind of vengeance, she's only getting more agitated.

"What did he do to her?" She sways in anger as Aria's sobs are echoed in Addison's voice.

What did I do to her? To Aria?

I loved her the only way I knew how. My head feels light and everything I think I know means nothing.

I should have known it would never be okay. I'm too fucked up to keep a woman like her. To keep anyone at all. What did I do to her? I drove her to betray me, to threaten to kill me.

"What happens between them--" Daniel starts to try and defend himself, not me. Not the relationship I had with Aria. Because there is no defending that. I know it deep in my gut.

I try to take a step forward, toward the door to get out, but stop when Addison shrieks at Daniel, shoving him away as he tries yet again to go to her.

"Please, just go!" Aria begs her and that only makes Addison more adamant at getting her out of the box.

As Addison screams at Daniel, I force my heavy and numb legs to move forward. "You knew! You knew what he was doing to her!"

The ice in my veins freezes my blood, and my heart refuses to beat without the warmth. "How could you?" she wails.

In a single day, everything has fallen.

Even as I walk out of the office, shutting the door behind me and hearing the faint screams leak into the barren hall, I know everything is ruined and nothing will be the same.

Everything is broken, and I have no way to fix a single piece of it.

It's all dashed beyond repair.

CHAPTER 4

Aria

THEY WEREN'T GOING to kill them. I want to think Carter and his brothers would never do that. *They wouldn't execute my family in front of me.* It's all I keep thinking as my eyes burn in the darkness of the box.

Nikolai would do it, though.

He would kill the Cross brothers, all of them, to set me free. But he doesn't know them and everything that happened. I haven't had a chance to convince him otherwise; all he knows is that I was taken. With every second that passes, I calm my panic, knowing I have to talk to Nikolai and stop this. I need it all to stop and for them to listen to me. For one of these thick-skulled men to just listen to me.

None of this would be happening if they listened to me.

A shuddering breath forces my body to tremble against the rough wood and my neck arches with a sudden deep breath.

I don't know if it's a panic attack or a sharp break from reality that's making me shake like I am.

Or the fear. The raw and paralyzing fear of what I know Carter is capable of and what I think he's going to do to me when I step out of this box.

"I love you," I whimper again, closing my eyes tightly and forcing the words out. I wish I could take it all back, but the alternative was watching my family die right in front of me. Watching Nikolai get shot in the back of the head. I cover my hot face with my hands, shaking my head like a lunatic at the thought.

"I don't want anyone to die." My strangled words are barely heard as the box shakes and then a hand bangs against the top.

"Aria, please." Addison's tone is desperate and I'm so ashamed. I don't want to leave this box. I feel like a child again, hiding in the closet and telling myself it's not real if I don't come out. If I stay here, none of this is real.

"He hurt you?" she asks, but her question is more of a statement. The question comes from a friend to a friend. Directed at a woman hiding from someone, someone she loves and crying hysterically. A grown ass adult, hiding in a box. I know exactly how this looks, but I don't know how to explain it to her, so she'd understand. She's not from this world. And she doesn't know Carter like I do either. Although, none of that makes this right. None of it. "How long has he been doing this?" Her voice breaks at the question and I hear her cry for me.

I wish I could die right here.

"Come out!" she screams to me, her voice sounding ragged as she thumps on the box.

I know we're alone; Jase made Daniel leave and I heard the door shut what feels like hours ago but is probably only minutes. It's only Addison in the room now, crying as she holds the box and apologizes to me as if she's done anything wrong at all.

"He wouldn't listen to me," I whisper to no one in the darkness of the box. Every time I tried to explain, he wouldn't hear me out. He'd cut me off and tell me to get out. Just like she is. At this point, I don't think there's a defense I could possibly have that would make what I did forgivable in Carter's eyes.

"Get out!" she yells even louder. Her voice sounds hoarse at this point, and I hear her lay her body over the box heavily, falling onto it and crying. "How could he do this?" she whispers and then sniffles. I don't know if she's talking about what Carter did to me, or how Daniel allowed it and defended it. I know to see him in this light... it changed how Addison sees him, and that fucking kills me.

"I never meant for this to happen," I tell her weakly, closing my eyes and feeling them burn from hours of straining to see in the darkness and shedding hot tears.

I can hear her move again, but I don't know what she's doing, and her voice doesn't travel far. "I'm so sorry. I didn't know… I didn't know."

Reaching up slowly, I force my numb fingers to unlock the box with a loud click that makes my heart pump hard, so hard it feels like it'll stop beating altogether.

As I lift open the top, the light filters in and I squint. It fucking hurts. My eyes feel like they're burning, but I force the top open further as Addison stands up in front of me on shaky legs and wraps her arms around me. I hold her back tighter, gripping on to her and bunching the thin cotton of her shirt in my hand as she pulls me hard into her chest. "It's not your fault," is all I can say, and the words are so flat, so lacking to my ears, that I harden them, pulling her back and staring into her forest green eyes.

"You did nothing wrong," I tell her.

She stands there with a troubled expression, wiping away her tears and shaking her head. "What did he do to you?" she asks me softly, still holding on to me as I climb out of the box on shaky legs, staring at the closed door. I feel cold; it's so cold.

There's not a piece of me that doesn't think Carter's watching. I know he must be. My first instinct when thinking he knows I'm out of the box is to hold myself. To wrap my arms around my shoulders and wait for him to punish me. I can barely stand looking at the closed door.

Addison grips me with a bruising force, shaking me until I stare into her eyes. "What did he do to you?"

I just want to cry. I don't know where to start, but the shame clogs my throat and keeps me from speaking at all.

"It's okay to tell me," she whispers although the words barely come out. Fresh tears leak from the corners of her eyes as she speaks so calmly to me. "Whatever he did, you can tell me. It's okay."

"It's my fault," I start, and an awful gasp leaves her as she covers her mouth. It hurts, everything hurts, but the way she looks at me like I'm wounded, and I don't know any better, I can't explain the pain it causes.

She shakes her head violently, staring back at me.

"You don't understand," I try to reason with her but my voice cracks and all I can think is to keep repeating that it's my fault. It is, truly.

"I knew he'd hate me. I knew…" I can't finish the sentence as the door to the office opens. Fear spikes through me and I jump back, hitting the back of my legs against the box and nearly tumbling in. Addison guards me against whoever enters as if she's my protector.

"Get out!" she sneers at whoever's entered and with equal amounts of curiosity and terror, I peek over her shoulder. Even though I'm feeling weak and pathetic, my fingers numb and my chest heaving in air.

It's only Daniel.

"Addison, please." Daniel's eyes are red-rimmed, and I'm shocked. "Let's get out of here, okay?" He talks softly with his hands held up, approaching us like the two wounded animals that we are. "We can leave," he offers her.

"I'm sorry," I say and can barely get the words out, seeking Daniel's gaze so he knows I mean it. "I'm so sorry." My voice is wretched.

"Look at her." Addison's voice ricochets in the office as she steps toward Daniel. "Look at her!" she screams in his face and he lowers his head, shaking it and trying to speak. Addison doesn't understand; all she sees is the pain. And there's so much of it.

"It wasn't my place," Daniel tells her sternly, but his expression is begging her to understand. How can she, when she knows nothing?

"She's not okay and your brother did this to her." She takes another step forward and points to me, still standing behind her. Her bottom lip trembles as she shouts, "You did nothing!" I grip on to my shoulders tighter and feel so small. It's hard to know what to think anymore, but I know what she sees, and it breaks my heart.

"He didn't have a choice--"

"Bullshit!" she cuts him off, screaming louder and louder, "You let him hurt her!"

Silence compresses the time, forcing the clock to tick faster. The moment passes quickly as my head feels woozy and I can't stop my breathing from coming in just as fast.

I hold onto myself tighter, struggling to remain upright.

"I'm leaving and I'm taking her with me." The anger is gone; there's only resolve in Addison's voice. "So help me God, if you stand in my way, I'll never come back to you. Never, Daniel."

"You're leaving me?" he asks, the look in his eyes hardening, the silvers sparking even as the tremors of intense emotion run along his hard jaw. His determination is still there, still unyielding.

"How could I stay with you?" she asks, trying to disguise the misery in her tone as she hurriedly wipes away the tears. "How could I stay here, knowing this?"

Any semblance of anger vanishes from Addison, the realization of what she's doing breaking through her rage and disgust. She's leaving him.

"Don't do this," I finally speak, pushing forward and grabbing Addison's arm. I plead with her, "You don't need to get in between; you don't need--"

"It's not about what I need to do," Addison speaks so softly, but with an evenness that's at odds with her disheartened expression. "It's about what I want to do." Her voice doesn't waver as she turns to Daniel, grabbing my hand in hers and telling him once again, "I'm leaving and I'm taking her with me." With a quick intake of air and tears brimming in her deep green eyes, she hesitates but then adds, "Don't follow me, Daniel."

"You know I will," he tells her with no remorse, but also with no objection to her leaving either.

My hand feels so cold in Addison's and I try to speak again, but she shushes me. "Please, don't make this harder on me," she speaks to me although it sounds like a desperate prayer.

It's quiet for so long, the agony lingering in the air. My gaze darts between the two of them; he's staring at her, but she's staring at the open door.

"I need to leave," she tells him again, squeezing my hand and I squeeze back, for her. I keep praying to hear Carter's footsteps or his voice. Any part of him to come to me and fix this. To fix the mess I caused.

"I don't want this to happen," I say, and the words are rough beneath my breath as I tug at Addison's hand for her to look at me. And she does. I can feel Daniel's eyes on me, but I don't look at him; instead, I beseech Addison, willing her to believe me. "He didn't know," I lie. I'd tell a thousand lies to keep it from tearing the two of them apart.

I can see Daniel shift uncomfortably out of the corner of my eye, but I don't react. Addison's expression turns soft and sympathetic as she squeezes my hand again. "You don't have to lie for them." Her voice is coated with a sadness that claws at my insides. She gives me a soft smile that's false and it falters when she tells me, "They're big boys and they knew what they were doing." Turning to Daniel she adds, "He knew I would never be okay with something like this." The emotion wrecks each of her words and in turn, the hardness of Daniel's gaze. I can't bear to look at him, watching as her words destroy them and whatever love was left between them.

"It's over. And I want out," she says in two breaths

that linger between them. "Let me go, Daniel. Please. You need to let me go this time." Even as the tears fall down her cheeks, she stands strong. I look past Daniel, refusing to look at either of them as my vision blurs with tears. The pain I feel for them magnifies as I realize she's taking me with her, and Carter isn't here at all.

He's not fighting for me.

He doesn't want me anymore.

I cover my face, pulling my hand away from hers and letting out the tortured sorrow of leaving him, but in the back of my mind I hear the voices hiss, he won't let it happen. She won't be able to leave so easily.

They're silenced with Daniel's only parting words. "I'll have Eli take you."

He doesn't touch her; he doesn't wait for a second longer. Instead, he simply turns and leaves us without another word, which only makes the pain grow stronger.

Carter, please, come take me. Please.

Addison struggles to control her composure, watching Daniel leave without even a single goodbye.

"I'm so sorry," I tell her again, hugging her back as she hugs me tight.

"You keep apologizing when this isn't your fault." Her words are soft and interrupted by the sound of footsteps.

I barely peek at the man named Eli, dressed in a fitted gray suit, no tie or cufflinks which makes it seem more casual, and with worn black dress shoes that are scuffed but somehow suit him.

It's his gaze that forces me to look away. Sharp pale blue eyes that have nothing but sympathy in them.

I don't want it. I'm ashamed as Addison leads me behind Eli and another man called Cason.

He's shorter than Eli, but not by much, and with bulging muscles that make him seem larger. He's the one who carries two bags he says are for us, but I don't know what's in them. Addison cries harder although she nods her head. Her strength at this moment is something I admire. I wish I could move forward, to make the decision to leave even knowing what the Cross brothers are capable of.

With Cason behind and Eli in front, our footsteps echo in the quiet hall. At every corner, I both hope that Carter is there to stop me and pray that he's not, so I can escape and hide away from him.

Every second closer to the door feels like it pulls on my torn heart.

Carter never comes, and that makes the chill from outside that much colder.

The peonies have died from the season's passing, they never last long, and the pale moon is full, illuminating every bit of the path to the sleek black sedan waiting for us even though the night is still early.

As I stare up at the house, searching for Carter in any of the windows, Addison waits for me to get in the car with silent tears still falling. He's not there. He's not watching.

"We don't have to leave," I tell her softly once more, desperately wanting Carter to come out and say he understands and that he forgives me. As I do him. In every way.

For what happened in the cell. For what happened today. It's all fucked up and there isn't an ounce of good in any of it, but I swear I love him. And love is forgiveness, isn't it?

I forgive him for anything he's done. I just want him back. I want him to love me again.

Please, Carter.

But not seeing him here... Him knowing that I'm leaving, and not bothering to say goodbye or try to fight for me in the least, I know he doesn't want me. It crushes me.

That thought is what forces me into the car, my back hitting the leather with a forceful blow. The sound of the trunk opening and the murmurs from Addison and Eli speaking mean nothing.

I don't know where I'll go or what I'll do.

My skin is numb, and I can barely breathe.

How many times have I tried to run? Yet here I am, and I would give anything for Carter

to stomp toward us and rip me from my savior to throw me back into the cell.

The leather seats protest as Addison gets in and buckles her seatbelt. I talk over the click. "I love him," I say, swallowing thickly. "I love Carter."

She barely glances at me, her eyes red and blotchy and her cheeks still flushed from crying.

"I love Daniel too." Her voice is hoarse as she leans her head back, resting it and staring at the ceiling of the car. "But love isn't enough sometimes. They can't do that to you."

I'm ashamed at her reply. I'm ashamed that I need saving.

I'm ashamed that I allowed it and with a single moment, she's seemingly put an end to it.

I wish I could rip my heart out and never feel love again. How easy life would be if you could truly be heartless.

Hours ago, I was in love with a man I know I should never have let near me.

And now he's watching me leave with zero objections, and it destroys me. I've never felt pain and regret like this. It doesn't matter what happened between us today; I would be feeling this tear in my soul regardless of what I'd done.

I should have known the concept of a happily ever after would never come to fruition when my last name is Talvery.

CHAPTER 5

Carter

SHE'S REALLY LEAVING.

She walked away. Straight through the front door. Never would I have seen it happen that way. She was always running and hiding in the shadows. I knew she'd leave one day, deep down in the pit of my stomach, but I never imagined it'd be like this. I never imagined it would fucking hurt like this either.

Swallowing thickly and ignoring the pain, I pick up another book from the floor, a hardback of *Lord of the Flies*. It's a collector's edition and I watch as I trace the spine of it with my fingers while asking Daniel, "Did you call Sebastian?"

He's leaning against the windowsill, but I can't fucking watch them leave like he is.

I won't watch her walk away from me.

"He knows already." His voice is low, not filled with the resentment I keep waiting for him to throw at me.

For being the hard man he is, Daniel always has forgiveness for his family. I wish I felt the same.

"How is that even possible?" I ask him while placing the book on the shelf and reach down for another. Someone else could take care of this and clean up my mess, but I don't want them to. I need to do something mindless before I deal with the consequences. Every time I bend down is another deep breath. Every book on the shelf is a piece put back into place.

I need to do this before I can deal with Jase going behind my back and everything that's happened over the last few hours. No one will come out unscathed. No. One.

Grinding my teeth together, I keep my back to Daniel as he answers me.

"Addison was ready to run; I could see it." He looks full of guilt and remorse as he stares out of the window, watching the car lights die in the thick of the forest as they move farther along the road.

Taking them away from us.

Taking her away from me.

Even glancing at the lights, so small and faint in the distance, shoves the knife deeper into my chest.

"So, I called him and asked if he would mind." He shrugs, attempting to refute the devastation of what's happened. It's clearly written in his expression, but he continues, "He's never used it and it's close, it's contained, and easily defended."

"Do they really think we'd let them go?" I ask him, feeling a surge of control again. She's never leaving me. Never.

"I'm sure Addison knows better." The urgency in Daniel's voice compels me to look back at him. He's leaning against the window now, facing the door to my office and staring at it aimlessly. "She'll try to leave, so we need to watch for that too."

"Always watching..." I mutter and then add, "For enemies coming and for our women leaving."

"Look at you, even now you care about her," he points out and Daniel's remark catches me off guard. "More than you admit to her."

"I just don't want them to have her."

A withering, sad smirk tugs at Daniel's lips, making him look even more miserable. "Our women." He repeats my words and the tension tightens around my chest. "Is there a difference with what's between Addison and me, and Aria and you?" he asks me in a voice laced with accusations.

"I love Addison," he tells me before I can answer, his breathing quickening as he struggles to hide the pain of watching her leave him.

He looks at the floor for only a moment, shoving his hands into his pockets before looking up at me and asking me outright, "Do you still love her?"

A beat passes, but only one. A single beat inside my chest and I know the answer. I breathe the word at the same time as the door opens and one of my men enters.

"Boss," Jett calls out my title while knocking on the open door.

"Do you have an update?" I ask him with an eyebrow cocked, looking at his knuckles on the door and wondering why he fucking bothered to knock.

Nodding his head and straightening his shoulders, Jett answers me without hesitation. Daniel's restless, leaning against the window then kicking off of it as he listens to the soldier. Jett's one of Eli's men. Eli's a lieutenant, the rank given to the men we trust implicitly to lead other men in our crime family. And Jett's the soldier he left behind to see that everything fell into place with him gone.

The four of us, my brothers and I, we each have two lieutenants and the area we claim is split four ways. It keeps things clean and organized. All of the men who work for us call me boss though. I'm the one and only boss.

Yet this motherfucker listened to Jase. Jase gave an order that directly countered mine, which should have been absolute, and this asshole listened to him.

A tic in my jaw starts to spasm as I remember, feeling the heat and anger of what happened only hours ago stir hate into my blood once again.

I can see the moment Jett realizes I'm not over that little stunt. His pupils dilate, and he stutters over a word before talking faster. That's what happens when you're fucking scared.

45

I have to remind myself that they didn't know. Jase is the one and the only person responsible.

"Eli and Cason are in the first car, and there are three decoy cars even though there's no trace of anyone watching or following." He swallows, and I can hear the dry gulp of his throat as I imagine tearing it out.

Jase defied me.

They followed his orders and didn't know of mine.

I remind myself of that fact, bending down to snatch another book off the floor and rein in the rage. Someone needs to have the piss beat out of them for what happened.

Slamming the book on the shelf, I see Jase's face. He let them go. Everyone will know that she put a gun to my head because of him.

"Would you like me to help— "

"No," I cut him off in a single, low breath, devoid of any emotion.

"Does 'anyone' include Romano's men?" Daniel questions and I watch for Jett's reaction, setting another book on the shelf. "Or better yet, who knows where Aria and Addison are going and that they've left the premises? Name every single man."

"Eli and Cason's men, the ten of us," Jett's quick to answer him and then stands silently at attention again. His gaze darts between the two of us, waiting for any other question or orders. The way he stands is firm and upright, same as Eli. But there's a nervousness about him that I don't like.

"I want thirty men spread out on the blocks surrounding Sebastian's place on Fifth," Daniel tells Jett, although I know he's talking to me. "The Red Room is on the northern side, so that street is already handled, but the other three sides of our territory are lighter on men and closer to Talvery than I like."

"We need fifty," I correct him. The east and south sides need to have a second row. If Talvery's going to come for them, if my enemies find out where Addison and Aria are, I want more men.

"We can do fifty easy," Cason answers as if it was a question and not a demand. He continues, "We just need to pull back on the lower east side, closest to Crescent Hills." Jett licks his bottom lip as he looks past me, using his fingers to tally up men absently.

I take a moment to really consider him as he tells me that "place" is always causing problems, but if we back off the problems take care of themselves anyway. As in the people we tend to have to control in Crescent Hills, simply kill the people that cause them issues if we don't step in.

I know that he's right because it's where I'm from and that's how it was when I grew up, but it pisses me off. The idea that we can move out of areas we've only just begun to take over and let them kill each other off because it's not worth it… it hits me in a way that it shouldn't.

Only because it's a place I used to call home. I know that's why, but it doesn't help control the rage that boils inside of me.

"Fifty then," Daniel answers and crosses his arms. From here I can feel him looking at me, but I'm still focused on Jett as he rambles on about which men can go where. I'm going to start calling him Mr. Calculus if he doesn't shut the fuck up soon. My jaw is clenched so tightly I think my molars will crack from the pressure.

I could see me taking out my displeasure on Jett. I can already feel how his jaw would crack under my fist. It would take more than one punch without my brass knuckles.

"Carter," Daniel says, and it breaks the vision of me beating the piss out of this entitled fuck. An asshole who didn't grow up the way I did and doesn't give a fuck about anyone in that city.

"What?" I don't hide the irritation as the word comes deep from my chest.

"Put the poor book down," he tells me, glancing at the book I'm practically ripping apart in my hand. Slamming it into its place on the shelf, I run my hand down my face and then brace my hands against the carved wood details of the bookshelf. I stare at the empty place still waiting for the books to be replaced.

"Ever the fucking comedian," I mutter under my breath, trying to relax and shrug off the need to let all my rage out.

"Keep a watch on the two of them and tell us if they want to leave," Daniel gives Jett his orders, but what the dumb fuck says next pushes me over the edge.

"What if Aria wants to go home?" Jett asks, concern evident in his gaze.

"What's that?" I can feel my own gaze narrow in on him as I push off of the bookshelf. The room feels hotter, smaller, and adrenaline races through my blood.

The soldier doesn't pick up on my anger. He doesn't get that what he's suggesting is going to get his head bashed against the fucking wall.

"GET OUT," Daniel speaks up as I take two steps toward my prey.

Jett goes still at Daniel's command, looking back at him as if wondering if he heard right. "She's not going anywhere," Daniel tells him as he stalks forward, pushing his hand against my chest for the second time tonight. The harder, darker side of his soul shows as he grabs Jett by his throat and pushes him against the wall. So hard I hear a crack, although I'm not sure what it was that made the sickening sound.

Jett's body sags in Daniel's grasp.

"Both women will be there temporarily." Although they're of similar height, it feels as if Daniel's towering over Jett as he nods and quickly agrees with Daniel, staring him in the eyes and making sure his voice is clear.

"Of course. They're there temporarily. I know that."

"Make sure you don't forget that." Daniel's parting words are sneered as he releases Jett and the man struggles to steady his feet. "Get out of here." Watching him yell in Jett's face eases some of the tension. Only some of it.

Jett doesn't pause or wait for anything else from either of us. He must have some sense in him after all.

"I wanted to bash his head in," I tell Daniel as the sound of that fucker racing down the hall to get away dims.

"I know," Daniel says with his back still to me as he rolls up his sleeves. "That's why I had to do it."

The ticking of the clock marches steadily between his last words and his next. "With the war coming, we need all the men we can get."

CHAPTER 6

Aria

WHEN I HEARD Eli say we were going to a safe house, this wasn't what I was expecting.

It's on the far end of the city, away from the hustle and bustle, in a quieter area and close to Main Street with a few shops within walking distance. There are a few quaint houses that line the street, but nearly a quarter mile separates each of them on this street.

This isn't like the safe house my father has. This house is in plain sight, but it's built for war if only you look closely enough at the exterior.

The three-story building is made of stone, with a concrete fence around the property, covered in beautiful ivy. The front door is all steel but beautifully etched with what looks like a Celtic pattern. I only got a brief glimpse before I was led here to the second floor, and each floor seems to be self-contained, so multiple families could live here and never even see each other. I'm in absolute awe, although it doesn't take the pain away in the least.

The kitchen is open to the living room. The center of the room is focused around a stone fireplace with a darkly stained, reclaimed wood mantel. Its ruggedness matches the iron and spicewood chandelier. But it's at odds with the clean sleekness of the all-white kitchen, just behind us.

We're stuck here, with a large L-shaped chenille sofa and matching armchairs that hug the fireplace until the guards say otherwise.

"Only a few minutes," is what Cason said. But more than a few have already passed as we linger in the beautiful gilded cage.

I'm biting my tongue though; I don't dare say a word to Addison as I pace behind the sofa. Addison's still pissed, but it seems fake to me. Like she's just trying to be angry at being locked up here rather than being brokenhearted over what happened.

She's been staring for the last ten minutes at the clothes she dumped on the sofa, trying not to cry. I can't stand seeing her on edge like this.

I'm an asshole, but I'll admit I'm grateful to be distracted by her. If I was alone, I'd be huddled in a ball crying on the floor.

"This is bullshit," she grits out the words, still

staring at the clothes. "This isn't what I meant when I said I was leaving!" she screams to no one.

"He said it would only be a week or so, right?" I ask her carefully, trying to calm her down just the slightest.

She nods and visibly swallows before rolling her eyes, seemingly remembering that she's annoyed with being held here rather than given free will to leave.

"For our protection." Addison picks up a dress and balls it in her hands before throwing it back down on the sofa. Pushing her hair out of her face, she leans her head back and takes a deep breath. She does that a lot, the leaning her head back and deep breaths. I've seen her do it a few times when she gets worked up.

"Is that like a meditation practice or something?" I ask her, wanting to change the topic if I can, to something... less devastating. I'm exhausted from crying, but tired of being exhausted from crying. I don't want to hurt right now; I need a distraction for just a moment. Just a moment to breathe before I face my reality again.

She nods her head, barely moving from the position and takes a moment before telling me, "It's a yoga thing, really, I don't know that I can meditate." She reaches for the duffle bag on the floor and picks up the clothes on the sofa, one piece at a time, to toss them back in. "My mind is always wandering, and I have to get up and do something."

I nearly smile, happy that she's talking to me about something else. It was silent in the car ride here and the tension has been suffocating me.

"Yeah, I get that," I answer her. "I tried meditation a while ago and it was not my cuppa."

"Cuppa?" she questions with her brow furrowed, and I stifle a small smile at her curious expression.

"Cup of tea." I shrug and add, "It wasn't my cup of tea." Staring at my own duffle bag on the armchair, I add casually, even as I feel the weight of my heart seem to grow and sink into my stomach, "I like tarot cards better."

"Oh!" The excitement in Addison's voice is not at all what I was expecting. Maybe she's better at pretending life is all right when it's in shambles than I am. "And like palm readings?"

I have to smile at her enthusiasm.

She keeps talking as she finishes gathering the clothes. "I went to see a gypsy in New Orleans once." She peeks over at me as I walk closer, taking a seat on the far end of the sofa. I have to, so I can hear her over the sound of the guards still walking through the safe house to make sure everything is in place. As in, cameras. I know those fuckers are putting up cameras.

I have to keep my mouth closed, my teeth grinding against one another at the thought, and keep the anger from showing as she tells me her story of the woman she met by Café du Monde. I swallow thickly as she tells me about New Orleans, a place I've never been.

She's still feigning an upbeat attitude and I'm trying to keep up. I wonder if she can pretend like this when she lies down. When there are no distractions and sleep evades her. Just the thought of what my mind will do to me tonight, makes me grab the throw blanket on the sofa and wrap it around me as if it could protect me.

"I wanted to get my coffee grounds read and all that too, but I didn't have time."

"Seven kids?" My brows haven't moved from their raised position since she casually mentioned that little fact the palm reader told her. "She said you're going to have seven kids?"

I didn't hear the rest of what she said about the reading as I stared off absently, pretending to listen but really thinking about tonight and how I know I'll cry again. I feel helpless, hopeless, and pathetic.

Addison's expression pales and she purses her lips before she carefully says, "Pregnancies." She doesn't hide the pain in her eyes when she clarifies. "She said seven pregnancies. She also said they wouldn't keep."

Fuck. I can't even look her in the eyes as I struggle to tell her I'm sorry. She only shrugs it off before pulling up on her bag to close it.

The sound of her zipping up the bag is accompanied by the sound of Eli walking back into the room. With his dress shirt sleeves rolled up, the tattoos on his arm are on full display. They're all in black and white with lots of detail. A compass that fades up his left arm catches my attention, but the tone of his voice brings my gaze up to his.

"The rooms are ready. We'll be downstairs at all times." Eli's blunt and has a hint of some accent. Irish or British maybe, I can't tell. It's subtle, but it's there.

"I don't want to stay here," Addison tells him again. Her shoulders rise and fall quickly as her breathing quickens. "I'm not with Daniel anymore." Her voice cracks, but she continues, "And I don't need a safe house. I need to leave."

Eli's expression is unmoving. I almost question if he's heard her as the silence stretches between them. The only sounds are from the other men behind Eli in the hall as they walk downstairs to their section of the safe house. "I understand." Eli's initial response takes Addison by surprise. She even flinches slightly, but then he adds, "There are some precautions that need to be taken first. But in one week, give or take, we will take you to wherever you want to go, and leave you alone."

Alone.

I hate that word.

"So, we're supposed to stay locked up in this fucking house?" Addison's anger rises as she asks the question, each word getting louder than the last. I watch as her blunt nails dig into her palms as she fails to rein in her anger.

"Main Street has several shops and a few restaurants. We have no objections to you walking the block... however, someone will be with you at all times."

My mind has been reeling all night with everything that's happened. I've been here for nearly two hours, and I'm only just now realizing why we have to stay here under house arrest with guards for one week. *And then we can go free.*

One week.

"He's going to kill them." With my gaze fixed on the sheer curtain, draped in the moonlight from outside the window, the crushing feeling in my chest returns. "One week until the war is over."

Addison turns slowly to face me, and I sink back further into the sofa.

"I'm being held hostage until my family is dead." My throat closes slowly like it's suffocating me, and my eyes burn hotter as the pain diffuses through me.

I've lost Carter. I've lost the chance to influence him because I failed.

And now I'm trapped in this beautiful place while everyone I love is murdered. My vision is blurred as I picture the house I grew up in, the blood on the walls, bullet holes in the doors. Licking my lips, I taste my salty tears. "Eli, can you answer me a question?" I ask him with a short breath I'm barely able to hold on to.

The lightheadedness floods my mind as he nods his head, yes.

"Is there someone to clean up everything you leave behind?" I struggle to breathe as I look him in the eyes and continue, "Or when I ask to go home in a week, will I be the one who has to clean up the bodies of my family?" My voice shakes on the last word, but he hears me. I know he does.

I picture my cousin, Brett, and his wife and their baby. In a moment, they're right where I last saw them during the holidays. And in a blink, they're lying dead on the floor, their eyes staring back at me as if seeing me for who I really am.

And I hate what they see.

Some of my family may be cruel like Carter, but not all of them are and so many people will die. I know what to expect. I've seen it before. I can't sit here and do nothing.

I refuse.

Eli stares back at me, assessing me and judging me, but I don't care. As long as I can hold on to the strength of my mentality, I don't care what he thinks. Knowing I can't and won't sit by and do nothing is all that matters.

"I know it's war, but I would rather be with them right now," I tell Eli, brushing the tears away as I realize that's where my place is. "I think it would be best if you sent me back to my home."

"Maybe when the week is over, you'll want to go somewhere else," is all Eli gives me.

It's not until he's gone that I realize Addison is silently crying.

She can't even look at me, but I don't care.

I don't care about anything anymore.

"It's what this life is like," I tell her solemnly, remembering all the nights the men would fill the kitchen downstairs, clinking their beers and patting each other on the back. "I had an uncle named Pierce." I haven't thought about it in forever, but now I'm reliving a certain night when I was fifteen years old. The night that marks the first time I fully grasped what my family did for a living and began to really see the consequences that came with it. I can feel how raw my throat is when I pause to swallow. From screaming, from crying.

"I came downstairs while he was holding something up in the air and everyone else in the room was cheering." Their voices echo in my head. "I remember smiling, so happy that my father was in a good mood." I don't know if she's listening, but I keep talking.

"My uncle was so happy to see me." I remember the way his grin widened before putting down whatever it was he'd been holding and hugging me like he hadn't seen me in years. "I felt like a part of the family that night. My father even gave me a small glass of wine despite the fact I was only sixteen." I remember the way it tasted, and how I felt when he poured from his bottle and gave me the glass in front of everyone. "He said, tonight we drink. Tonight, we celebrate Talvery. And everyone cheered again when I took a sip."

I peek over at Addison, who's listening intently and waiting for the punch line.

"It wasn't until a few days later that Nikolai told me it was a human tongue. The tongue of a rat who was murdered, and they were celebrating because the charges were dropped with no witness living to testify." I had to beg Nik to tell me; he told me I wouldn't want to know, but I pressed him. After he told me, I knew I could trust his opinion if I ever wanted to know something again.

I stare at the fireplace, wishing it would crackle with a soothing flame, but it's empty and there's no wood here to start a fire.

"Talverys and the Cross brothers are the same. And they'll both kill each other or die trying." It's a truth I've wanted to avoid for so long, but now it seems as if I can only try to limit the damage they'll cause.

"That's not the way they grew up," Addison tells me with tears in her eyes. "They were good people."

"My family is full of good people too." My gut churns from trying to defend this life to her. To someone who didn't grow up in it. "They just do bad things. Like my uncle. He loved his wife, he loved his kids, and he would have done anything for me if he were still alive."

It's quiet for a moment as Addison slowly sits down next to me, holding onto herself like she'll fall to pieces if she doesn't.

She doesn't speak for a long time; neither of us does. But neither of us gets up either. "I don't understand how Daniel got into this. This isn't what they were like before. I swear to you. They were good and... and... I don't know how this happened." She looks lost like she had no idea. I've seen women before who are in denial, who turn a blind eye. But she's truly shocked. Maybe she didn't realize how real this life can be. How close to death it is.

"I do."

My response grabs her attention and she waits for

more, but I don't know how much she really wants to know, or what she needs to know.

"For the longest time, there wasn't anyone south of Fallbrook. That's where I'm from and basically the territory my father keeps. My father talked about taking it a lot." I remember back when I was little, how I'd sit in his office coloring and he'd have hushed conversations about the developments in Back Ridge. "There wasn't anyone living there, no businesses, but then," I clear my throat and tell her, "then developments grew and there were more people. More opportunities, as my father called it."

"He and Romano had two territories side by side, and both wanted it. But the areas are like a cross, sort of." Four quarters, I draw it out on the blanket on my lap, the way Nikolai explained it to me. "Carter's area is the bottom left, but his portion is bigger now. The bottom right is Crescent Hills and it's not claimed, just a shit town with no one policing it, no one protecting it. Carter and his crew keep moving closer and closer, but they only take it little by little. My father has the upper left and Romano the upper right. They both wanted the territory where Carter is now, but while they waged a cold war against each other because of my mother…" I swallow a dry lump not knowing if she knows but not in a state to explain. "Carter took over. One by one, killing the men who worked for my father who tried to stop him, or, sometimes, Carter took on my father's soldiers, proving he would be ruthless and that the area was his, but he had mercy for those who stayed with him."

"So, it was Carter?" she asks, and I can see in her eyes she doesn't want to believe Daniel was involved.

"I've heard Jase and Carter's names a lot." I almost say more, but I hold it back, swallowing my words. "But Carter is the one name that everyone knows. It's either Carter or the Cross brothers."

Addison's brow is pinched but her expression is riddled with anguish as she says, "I don't know why Carter would do that. I don't know why he'd want to live this way."

Again, I almost say, "I do," but I don't. It's because my father knew what Carter was capable of. He knew they would take over. My father tried to kill them before they could become the powerful family they are now, but he failed. His failed attempt is what made Carter who he is.

The truth, and facing the truth, causes a coldness to flow across my skin and I pull the blanket more tightly around me.

"I understand if you could never be friends with someone like me. Someone whose family makes a living through death and sin. Someone who..." I trail off, pausing for a moment before what I'm about to say next. I have to close my eyes to say, "Someone who broke you and Daniel up."

"Stop it," Addison breathes the command with a seriousness I wasn't expecting. "You didn't break us up and you're still my friend." She grips my hand in both of hers as I stare back at her, hoping she still feels this way in the morning. Because I have no one right now and, in a week, I may have even less than no one.

"It's going to be okay and we're going to look out for each other. You have to look out for the ones you care about. You know?" Her gaze begs me to agree with her, to stay strong. But I'm not like Addison.

Tears beg to run down my face, but I bite them back, refusing to cry any more tonight. Instead, I nod my head and force out my reply, although the words are strangled. "I'm trying to. But what can I do when the ones I care about want each other dead?"

The silence comes again, but she's quick to end it this time.

"Let's have a drink." She's off the sofa before I can even tell her how badly I need one.

I can only nod my head in agreement, still wrapping my head around the spiral of horrific events that led me here.

I can't think about anything but Carter as I hear her open a bottle of wine and the glasses clink on the counter. Instead, all I can do is picture Carter's face the exact moment I lost his trust and he lost his fucking mind.

It's going to haunt me forever.

If not that, then the sight of my family in coffins.

There was no way for me to win.

I don't want to do this anymore. I can't deal with this anymore.

I need to stop this.

CHAPTER 7

Carter

IT'S QUIETER HERE than I thought it would be. Sebastian picked a nice area. He had the place built two years ago but never came back. I don't know if it's the memory of him or everything that happened tonight that makes my heart twist like someone's wringing it out from inside my chest.

The whiskey didn't make the pain better. Not the first glass, not the second. Not when I threw the bottle at the window, shattering it and filling the room with the smell of liquor. Earlier, I spent too long sagging against the wall while sitting on the floor of the office staring at the box. The box that's still open, empty, and pushed up against the rug. I can't move it back. I can't bring myself to move it back as if she was never in there.

Everything is telling me to let her go.

Logic and reason. She will never love me because of the way we started. She will never love me after I kill her family. She will never love me, because of the man I am.

I know it all to be true.

But the idea of letting her leave fucking hurts.

"Do you want me to go in with you?" Daniel asks me from the driver's seat, ripping my gaze from the front of the house and cutting through my thoughts.

"Are you sure you're okay to see her?" he asks me the real question.

"I'm not going to hurt her," I tell him as I stare back at the house, praying I'm telling the truth. I want her to feel this pain. I want her to know how much it hurts.

"What are you going to do?" he asks me, his hands sliding down the leather steering wheel.

"I'm going to give her what she wants," I lie. I'll never let her leave me.

My brother's voice is stern and loud in the cabin of the car as he says, "You're making a mistake."

I'm taken aback by his criticism, staring at him as the dark night sky gets darker. "You can do what you'd like with Addison; I won't judge you. But stay out of it when it comes to me and Aria." It's all I can tell him because I don't know what to do with Aria. I don't know what I can do with a woman who would betray me like she did.

"Are you really going to let her walk away?" When I don't answer his question, he pushes me by saying, "She'll have no one when this is done with. No one."

I raise my voice to reply and end this conversation. "I said I'm going to give her what she wants. I didn't say I'd let her go." My blood rushes in my ears as Daniel's eyes narrow in the darkness.

"Are you coming in?" I ask him, refusing to let him continue.

"No, she's not inside. She walked down to the liquor store for more wine when Aria went to bed." He settles back in the seat and looks straight down the road to add, "I'm going to drive up there and keep an eye on her from a distance."

Pausing, he looks at me before adding, "Cason's with her and there are eyes are on her, but still…"

"She must know you'll be watching her," I say absently, remembering everything that happened months ago.

His nod is solemn. "I know she does. I'm sure she hates it too."

Giving him a tilt of my head to part ways, I grab the handle to open the door, but Daniel's words stop me. "I wonder if she'll know when I get to her."

With my fingers wrapped around the handle, I still, then ask, "What do you mean?"

"She used to know somehow. Years ago, when Tyler died. Every time I came close to her, she'd turn around as if she knew I was there. It didn't matter how far away I was or how many other people were around us. She always knew, back then."

He finally looks over at me, the sorrowful smirk still on his face. "I wonder if it'll be the same even now."

I don't know what advice to give my brother. I can feel his pain and there are no words to help him.

"Just make sure she's safe," I tell him, remembering all those years ago and everything that happened between them... between all of us.

"Always," he tells me and smacks the back of his hand against my arm. "Don't fuck it up." He forces a weak smile to his face, although it doesn't reach his eyes. I can't give the same back to him.

The sounds of the night greet me as the car door opens and then shuts easily. The crickets and the wind are all I can hear. The men posted on the side of the building see me and I acknowledge them with a simple nod. I button my suit jacket and walk up the sidewalk and onto the porch. With every step, the anxiety over my fears grows. The fear that I've lost her forever. That she never loved me, and I never really had her. The fear that tonight has destroyed anything and everything that's between us.

There's no turning back from what's happened. There's no denying that she's clouding my judgment and keeping her means losing the confidence and respect from my men.

Helplessness is something I haven't felt in so long, but it's with me now as I stalk toward the safe house.

Eli's been at the front door all day with his earpiece

in and the phone displaying the monitors. He stands up straighter with the smack of my boots on the stone steps as I make my way toward him.

"Aria's in the north bedroom on the second floor. Addison's at--"

"The liquor store," I finish the sentence for him.

"Boss," he says and rewards me with the barest flicker of a smile. "Of course, you'd know." He opens the massive front door; it's solid steel eight feet high and three feet wide. The bright light from the foyer reflects off the freshly polished wood floors. It's been a while since I've been here and the memory of standing on this threshold with Sebastian makes me pause.

Chloe, Sebastian's wife, is the one who chose everything for this house. She wanted to come back. I really thought they were coming home years ago when this house was built, but they didn't.

Standing there, I remember my childhood like it was yesterday, back when I was a different person. Back before all that shit happened with Aria's father; before my best friend left and my mother passed away, leaving me on my own to take care of my drunkard of a father and my four brothers. I've never thought back on it and felt ashamed. But as I stand here, I think back to who I used to be and know I would hate the man I've become. I would hate who I've turned into and what I've done.

You can't go back though. You can never go back.

"Is there anything I can do for you?" Eli asks quietly, carefully.

"How is she?" I ask him. I've known Eli for four years now. He helped me take over the majority of this territory and he's the only reason I've moved deeper into Crescent Hills, where I'm from. There's no law in Crescent Hills, so moving my empire there is a task harder than most, and the income doesn't justify it. It's a hellhole no one wants, but I thought Sebastian would eventually come back and help me take it. I thought wrong.

"She's been crying on and off since Addison left." Eli's gaze doesn't stay on mine as he reports on Aria to me. He looks down at his shoes and swallows before looking me back in the eyes. "She saw some of the news. I'm not sure what she's most upset about. Leaving you or losing her family."

Anger is a slow simmer. I shouldn't have waited to pull the trigger. "If they were already dead, I wouldn't have this problem."

Eli nods in agreement. "We're ready when you are, Boss."

"Romano's already taking down the streets in the upper east."

Eli nods again and says, "It's been all over the news today. I imagine Romano will hit them from the south side this week."

"Talvery will be expecting it though."

"That's good for us here. Chances are good he'll take his men on the northernmost streets up there and hit him harder."

"They both react predictably."

"And they'll both fall… predictably." The grin on his face would be reflected on mine, but all I can think about is how Aria will truly hate me then. She was willing to threaten me to save them. Deep in my gut, I know the idea of vengeance is something that will cross her mind. And it fucking kills me.

"I don't know that I can ever trust her again," I speak the revelation out loud and regret it immediately. What the fuck is wrong with me?

"She'll get over it. I overheard her explaining things to Addison; she understands why this has to happen."

The night air clings to me, holding me here at the threshold instead of moving forward to face Aria.

"Where did you find that dumb fuck, Jett?" I ask him to get off the topic and remind him who I am. His fucking boss.

"He's a good shot, just a little shit when it comes to his mouth. I think he has Asperger's or something." He looks past me and into the night for a moment before continuing. "He's not too good at reading social clues, but in the war, he waited three days to get a shot on the insurgents in Afghanistan. Three days he stayed in the same bunker, barely bigger than a shack. He didn't fucking move until the three on his hit list were in his sights." He huffs a short laugh although it lacks genuine humor. "They came out for a smoke, thinking they were in the clear since it'd been quiet for three days. It only took him twenty seconds to get all three of them in the skull."

"I still want to rip his fucking throat out," I tell him

absently, although my respect for Jett grows as I picture what he's been through.

Eli shrugs. "I've told him before that he could still shoot his gun if I cut out his tongue." He chuckles and adds, "Jokingly, of course. I owe him my life."

"I'll keep that in mind the next time I want to punch his face in." My words come out dull, lacking the conviction I had before.

"What'd he say?" he asks me.

"Nothing," I answer him, knowing I don't want to have this conversation with him. I respect Eli, but he's not my friend. This is business.

He nods once, opening the door just a hair more and the soft sound of it creaking is loud in my ears.

"Tell the men not to go in and to stall Addison until I'm done in here," I say, staring at the spiral staircase that leads to the second floor where my little songbird is now caged. "I don't want her to hear this."

"Yes, Boss."

I pat him on the shoulder as I walk in, but I don't look him in the eyes. Even though I'm staring at the staircase, all I can see is everything that happened hours ago. The gun she pointed at me, the box she ran to and hid in. The sight of the car as it pulled away and how she didn't object.

My throat's tight and the hammering of my heart gets faster and more painful as I climb the stairs. The railing is slick under my hot palm.

She's mine.

She's going to know I fucking own her when I leave her tonight.

Even if she still leaves me, she will always belong to me.

Always.

The thought makes the rushing of blood in my ears that much louder. Each step closer to the door my cock gets harder, thinking of every reaction she'll have to me.

Anger, hate even.

Or maybe she'll beg me to forgive her.

I close my eyes, resting the flat side of my fist against the wall to the right of her bedroom door at the thought of her begging me for mercy. Something she refused to do in the cell.

My eyes open slowly at the sound of the bed creaking from just beyond the door.

* * *

Aria

I HEARD his footsteps before the door opened.

I can't explain why I prayed for it to be Carter. The last time I saw him, all I had was fear of him.

With the window open, the wind drifts in, shifting the curtains out of place and letting the moonlight drape over Carter's dominant form.

72

My heart flickers in a weird uneven beat and I'm reminded of the first time I ever saw him. The same fear races through me, but so does the feeling that he could save me.

If only he wanted to, but from the sharp look in his eyes, that's not what he has planned for me at all.

At this point, I'm okay with that. He can do what he'd like to me because I already know I'll submit to him. I already know I still love him. No matter how fucked up it is.

"Carter," I whisper his name as I sit up in bed, letting the sheets fall into a puddle around me. A shiver graces my skin as the wind tickles my shoulder.

The floor creaks with his heavy step and the shadow across his face moves, hugging the sharp lines of his jaw as he stalks toward me.

"Get on your knees," he commands me in a rough voice. That's the only greeting he gives me and it reminds me of what life was like in the cell with him.

Defiance runs deep in my blood and it spikes anger high in my chest as my jaw clenches.

"That's what you have to say to me?" I question him with my voice wavering. Anxiety and heartbreak are equally present, making my toes curl and my fists bunch the silk sheets. I can barely breathe as I bite back the words, "You didn't come for me."

He pauses at the end of the bed, but only for a moment, a single beat of my wretched heart. He speaks softly, yet forcefully as he slips off his jacket and lays it carefully at the end of the bed.

"I have many things to say to you, Aria Talvery," he practically spits my name and I snarl back, "Fuck you," feeling the hate for him intensify.

I've always known he was my enemy, but I never felt as if he saw me that way. The tides have changed.

His deft fingers unbutton his shirt and my eyes leave his to watch as he strips.

"I told you to get on your knees," he reminds me in a voice that drips of dominance and sex. He tosses his shirt on top of his jacket, losing the control he had a moment ago.

My eyes are drawn to the leather of his belt as he unbuckles it and then quickly pulls it from its place, letting the leather hiss through the air.

My pussy clenches as he bends the leather into a loop and waits for me to obey him. "You've already questioned me, defied me, and lied to me today. Are you really going to disobey me again?"

I swallow thickly, knowing I want his punishment, and I want this. But I didn't lie to him.

"I've never lied to you and I never will," I tell him quickly, feeling my pulse quicken.

"You didn't tell me the truth. That's lying," he says, his voice louder and he doesn't hide his anger in the least.

"I won't..." I pause and trail off. Biting down on my lower lip, I hate that the one conflict we have that will tear us apart, again and again, is one we will never agree on. "I won't sit back and let you kill them. I won't."

Carter's movements are faster than I thought possible, sending a spike of fear through me. The belt hits the bed as he grips my chin and lowers his lips to mine. My heart races and lust mixes with terror. "You don't have a choice," he whispers against my lips.

I question myself even as the words leave my lips, "You're wrong."

I can feel his heat; I can hear his heart hammer in his chest as I stare into his dark eyes. I could get lost in them forever and at this moment, I wish I could. "I wish things were different," I tell him as his silence grows.

"They will be soon," he says. The darkly spoken words come with a threat. "On your knees, songbird."

It's his nickname for me, his grip on my chin, his lips so close to mine and the rapid pace of his heart, that all make me move.

I keep my eyes on his for as long as I can as I get onto all fours and let him slowly strip my pants from me. He pulls them down slowly, teasingly even as his fingers brush down my sensitive skin.

The cool air is all I can feel for a moment and I know the belt is coming. I brace for it, but there's nothing for what feels like forever.

"Do you think you deserve this?" he asks me with his voice low and not an ounce of resentment that I expect.

I breathe the word easily, truthfully, "Yes."

The belt bites the flesh of my right thigh from

behind and I scream out in agony. He didn't waste a second.

My thighs tremble as I try to stay on all fours.

Smack! The edges of the belt scrape against my ass and send a wave of pain through my body while burning where they slice across my skin. I can't control the sob that claws its way up my throat. My toes curl as I grip the sheets tighter and fight back the tears.

I jump at the soft touch of Carter's hand against my heated flesh, wishing I'd said no, but then I would be the liar I claimed not to be.

"Do you know what happens to men who point a gun at me, Aria?" Carter's voice is laced with a deadly threat as he bends over me, his hard cock digging into my ass and just the feeling of it sends a deep-rooted desire to surface in my blood.

The lust nearly drowns out the pain. It's so close, and I wish it would, but Carter isn't finished punishing me yet.

His lips brush the shell of my ear as he tells me, "They don't live to pull the trigger."

I have to swallow before I can answer him. My skin alternates between pain and pleasure on the places where his hand still rubs soothing circles. "I never would have pulled it," I answer him in a soft voice while rocking my hips back against him. I've always been a whore for him. I bow to him and love it. Some sick side of me desires it. I imagine I always will.

"You don't care that everyone saw, do you?" he asks me and the weight of what I've done feels heavier.

"I'm sorry. I didn't want to do it." I swallow thickly, conflicted by my exhaustion, my pain, my greed for more of his touch. "You left me no choice."

He pulls away instantly, leaving my body feeling the chill of the air between us. I can hear the metal buckle of his belt clink and see him raise his arm in the shadows that play on the wall in front of me.

I close my eyes tightly but it doesn't help in the least.

Smack! The belt bites at my left ass cheek, and then immediately moves to the right.

I bite down as hard as I can on nothing and try to hold back my cries as the belt screams in the air and lands blow after blow against my tender flesh.

My arms buckle as the pain rips through me. Tears leak uncontrollably from the corners of my eyes.

Carter fists the hair at the base of my skull and forces me to look at him.

His eyes are dark and swirling with tortured emotion. "I need to see you, Aria. You can't hide from me."

My head shakes before I realize I've moved, the stinging pain making even the small movement of brushing my thigh against his absolute agony. "I can't," I whimper.

I've never felt a pain like this. I try to hold back the tears as my shoulders shake, but they come regardless.

"You can take this," Carter tells me, grabbing the reddened flesh of my thigh and squeezing it. The pressure forces the pain to shred every last piece of control I have.

With his right hand on my thigh, he cups my pussy with his left.

My back bows instantly and I'd collapse to my side if he wasn't holding me in place. The pleasure is unimaginable. Every inch of my body feels it. My nipples pebble, but my neck arches and my body begs for more.

"You can take this, Aria." Carter's voice is gentle, soothing, and deep as he rubs his fingers against my sensitive clit. From the way he sounds right now, I almost wonder if the lust he once had for me is now gone, but I know that can't be true. That can't be the case from the way he starts to touch me.

He pinches my clit and a lightning bolt of pleasure thrills every nerve ending in my body. I'm hot and cold at the same time. Quivering beneath the man who gives me pain I can't bear and pleasure that's as equally consuming.

And I crave more of him. I need his fingers inside of me.

He pulls away as the numbing pleasure races through me and I see him reach for the belt again.

"Carter," I whimper a plea. I love the pleasure, but the pain is terrifying. "Please," I beg him.

He hesitates. With my cheek on the pillow, staring up at the broken man who only knows how to break others, I beg him again. "Please, forgive me."

"I've already forgiven you," are the only words he gives me before gripping the belt tighter.

I close my eyes, waiting for more punishment, waiting for Carter to take me how he thinks he needs.

Instead, a soothing hand runs along the dip in my waist, and as much as I want to pull away, knowing his gentle touch is going to cause where he's struck me to flare with pain, I stay still for him. I let him caress where the belt met my skin, and bring the pain to the surface even more.

"I just want you," I whisper into the pillow. It feels damp beneath my cheek, soaked from my tears. "Please, Carter."

"This is me, Aria. This is who I am."

His words are a fire that licks along the wounds of my heart, split into two halves of who I am. The first half of me is a woman who's broken and in love with a man who's been hurt more times in this life than I could possibly bear. And the other half is a woman who wants to be strong and refuses to allow her will to be ignored any longer.

"You don't know who you are anymore, Carter. No more than I knew who I was when I held the gun," I tell him in a shuddering voice. "Take from me what you want," I concede. Closing my eyes, I bury my head in the pillow but then remember what he said. And so, I position myself on all fours again, even as my legs shake. "I'll give it all to you."

The belt drops to the bed with a thud and before I can turn my head to look over my shoulder at Carter, he plunges deep inside of me, his cock filling me and stretching me without mercy. One of his hands grips my hip to keep me upright as the force of his thrust nearly shoves my body into a prone position from the blow. Fuck! It's too much so quickly. The scream that's torn from me is silent.

With his other hand, he pinches my clit hard and the force of the pleasure tearing through me makes my back bow as I scream out his name.

His thumb rubs my clit relentlessly as he rides through my orgasm, fucking me like it's the last thing he'll ever be able to do.

And I take it all. Biting down on the pillow to mute the screams and writhing beneath him from the mix of pain and pleasure that confuses my body, I take all of him.

Over and over again.

I take it until I think he'll break me. Until my body begs me to flee, but even then, he doesn't stop. He's a brutal man, with brutal instincts and I don't know that he'll ever have mercy on me again.

I'm barely sane, barely coherent when I feel his thick cock pulse inside of me. The head of his dick is pressed deep inside of me, and I've never before wanted a moment to last forever like I do now. Feeling the most intense orgasm I've ever had while Carter groans my name and then lowers his lips to kiss my shoulder.

He breathes heavily as he lays his chest on my back, moving one hand to brace himself and the other to hold my belly, keeping my skin pressed to his.

The last kiss he gives me is a long one, his lips to my shoulder. Like he doesn't want it to end.

"I fell in love with the idea of you," he whispers after pulling his kiss away from me. "Then I fell in love with fucking you." There's an agony etched in his words. It sounds like he's telling me goodbye and I've only just now realized it.

"Carter," I say as I turn in his embrace, ignoring the pain from the belt which is still present, bringing my hands to either side of his hard jaw and try to kiss him back, but he pulls away.

"I thought I loved you." Every bit of the man who brings terror to all who defy him is gone. There's a softness in his eyes that begs me to accept it all, to bow down to him and bend to his will. No matter what it is.

But I can't. Not anymore. Not after what happened, and I saw the truth of what's to come. And if that means this is the end…

I gaze into his eyes as he stares into mine, and I can feel the unspoken words. Either I submit to him, or I'm his enemy.

"I love you, Carter. But I won't be your songbird anymore. Not when you chose to ignore the one thing I need from you."

"You want me to surrender and that's something I can't do." He swallows thickly, the hard edge to his tone growing rougher. "You're making it impossible for us to be together."

The tension between us is too real, so thick and so suffocating. "So are you," I tell him. "I love you, but I will go to war against you." My words are shaky as they leave my lips. "I still love you, Carter. And I still want you." The last words come out rushed and I beg him to believe me.

"I will kill every man of the army that backs you, Aria. I will destroy them all until there's no reason left to fight." He doesn't mention anything about love. Only war.

"I will die to protect them," I tell him the truth. They're my family. And they've protected me. "I have to," I plead with him to understand.

He doesn't conceal the pain my answer causes him. And that only makes my own suffering grow. "Where is that loyalty for me? For my brothers?"

"I will never hurt them or you." The thought of them dying at the hands of my own family clutches my heart in a vise. My voice cracks as I speak, "I only said I would protect my own."

"Little naïve songbird... I wish you could."

CHAPTER 8

Aria

EVERY TIME I make even the tiniest of movements, the ache between my legs consumes my body.

I both hate it and love it. I love the reminder that Carter came for me; I hate that I'm again faced with the reality I can't outrun.

I've been watching the news and listening to the guards. I know blood has already been spilled. Yesterday I got a glimpse of it, but I wasn't sure. Today Addison's kept the news on and I know for certain the war has begun.

I recognize the names of some of the men in my father's army. The soldiers. Men who have gathered in my kitchen late at night. Men who have shared dinner with my family from time to time.

Men who have been kind to me.

Men who have looked after me when my father wasn't there.

Men who have children and wives.

And the names I don't recognize from men who live on the east side of the state… I imagine they have families too. Or did. Before this happened.

My father made me go to the funerals whenever someone died. Always. I've never missed any of them. He said they were family and deserved that respect. As much as I've hated my father and as much as I think I'm nothing but a bother to him, or maybe a bad memory of my mother, I always respected the dead and their families.

This time I won't be able to, and for some reason that hurts me deeper than I think it should.

Two names that haven't come up are Nikolai and Mika.

The first, a man who I've loved in more way than one.

And the second, a man I've dreamed of killing myself.

In this world, there are men who are good, and there are men who are evil. I won't be convinced otherwise. In war, both types of men die. And both types of men populate every army.

"How are you doing this morning?" Addison's question pulls my gaze from the coffee maker to her. I meant to turn it on and never did. I can't concentrate on anything else but the war.

She looks like she didn't get any sleep at all. The dark circles under her eyes are a dead giveaway. "I came in to check on you last night, but you were already asleep."

My lungs seize thinking how grateful I am that she didn't come in while Carter was there. I've never felt so torn in my life as I did last night. It's an impossible situation.

"Yeah, I passed out." I offer the lame excuse and it feels fake on my tongue knowing I'm hiding the truth from her. I finally hit the button to start up the machine but then have to check to make sure I added water. I did.

All the while, Addison heads to the fridge as if it's any other kitchen, knowing Eli fully stocked it last night.

I almost tell her Carter came over purely out of guilt, but I swallow my words. She won't understand. She clears her throat and speaks before I can confess though.

"I saw Daniel… that's what took me so long."

Unshed tears shimmer in her eyes and she slams the fridge door shut before tossing the butter on the counter so she has both hands free to press her palms to her eyes. "I'm sorry."

"You have no reason to be. Out of everyone involved, you have no reason to be," I say and wish she could understand how empathetic I am to her. "I get it. Let it out," I tell her while putting my hand on her shoulder and running it back and forth to try to soothe her.

"I just can't believe he'd be okay with the way Carter treated you. That he would do nothing."

I let out a long breath, understanding why she's standing so strongly against Daniel, but hating that I'm a part of that reason.

"I've come to terms with two things," I tell her, hoping it will help her. "One, I love Carter even if he hates me." The first confession brings her eyes to mine. "Two, I'm not going to sit back and do nothing. I won't ever let him do something that will hurt me or my family without fighting him."

"How can you be with him, knowing...?" She doesn't finish, but she doesn't have to.

"I don't know how. I honestly don't. And I don't know if any of it really matters." I lean my back against the counter and grip on to it from behind. "I can't stop this war. I can't protect everyone. I can't stop the people I love from dying." As I say the last part, my mother comes to mind and I try to block her out. I'm already spent with emotion and trying to balance right and wrong, love and war, that any mention of her will be my undoing and it's not even ten o'clock in the morning.

"This life is brutal," I whisper and then clear my throat to face Addison again. "But it's my life. And I want to be in control of my own decisions."

"You know we're still locked up, right?" Judging by the hint of a smile on her lips, her words are meant to make me laugh and they do, a small breath of a laugh.

Reaching for the butter and content to let the conversation die, she adds, "Let's eat before we think of how we're going to escape."

"I can hear you," a voice says from behind us and scares the shit out of me. Eli's in the doorway, a smirk on his lips and if he was closer I'd be tempted to smack it off his face.

"I'm sure you all can," I answer him and look toward the ceiling. "I haven't found the cameras yet."

He doesn't respond to my jabs as I watch the coffee maker sputter the last bit of my caffeine addiction into a ceramic mug. Instead, he tells me, "You have a message."

He's so tall, it only takes four strides for him to close the gap between us and reach me, holding out a folded piece of paper.

"Did you read it?" I ask him before taking the small piece of parchment.

His stare is hard and unforgiving as he answers, "Yes." Pissed off from the lack of privacy, I easily toss the precious piece of paper onto the counter. I have no idea who it's from, but I continue moving around my warden to look for sugar in the cabinets.

"Does Carter know?" I ask him when I finally find it. I close the door slowly, holding the box of sugar tighter than I should.

"Yes."

I nod and then ask, "Is it from him?"

I would be surprised if it was, since he didn't have much else to say last night, and Eli proves my assumption correct with a single word.

"No."

I swallow down the sudden pang of anxiety, wondering who it's from and what it says, but I don't dare let on to Eli.

"You don't have to hate me," he says as I continue to walk around him and Addison as she fries something on the stove.

"You don't have to hover," I answer him immediately.

Without another word, he leaves, and I feel guilty although I know I shouldn't.

"What are you cooking?" I ask Addison after he's left, staring at the piece of paper without reaching for it.

"Eggs, do you want some?" she asks, peeking at me and then at the paper. I'm surprised she doesn't ask about it; I can see the question in her eyes.

"Sure," I answer just to be friendly. I don't think I could eat if I tried though. I'm already sick to my stomach.

"How do you like them?" she asks before flipping her own in the pan.

"Over easy, please, and thank you," I tell her, trying to keep my voice upbeat and waiting to open the note until I'm alone.

"Yolk?" Addison makes a face. "Eww. Really I don't know if we can be friends anymore." She's only joking though. I know she is, but the thought of losing her sends a wave of nausea through me.

"Fine," I tell her back in as playful of a voice I can manage, "I'll eat them however you're making them. I like eggs however they come," I lie. I've only ever had eggs over easy. I don't even eat hard-boiled eggs. I can't justify why I lie to her or why I'm so nervous and feeling so alone. But I do and am.

"I can make them how ever." Addison shrugs and then adds, "Over easy is the easiest way anyway. I just don't like the taste of yolks."

Her easygoing reply settles the nerves still racing through me, but I glance back at the note and notice when her gaze follows me there. Still, she doesn't ask questions and I get the feeling that's a learned habit of hers.

I watch as she cracks two eggs on the side of the pan, then takes a bite of hers from a plate on the right side of the stove.

"I can totally cook them if you want to eat," I offer, feeling guilty. I can't shake all these awful feelings running through me.

"I like it," Addison tells me and then takes another bite. The pan sizzles as the tension runs through my shoulders and the note stares back at me.

"Can I tell you something else?" Addison asks me, scraping her fork on the plate rather than looking at me. When I don't answer she peeks up at me and I'm quick to nod my head.

"I like that they're here in a way."

"Who?" I ask her, feeling my forehead wrinkle with confusion.

"Eli and Cason." She doesn't hide the guilt in her tone. "I know they're basically keeping us hostage but seeing all those people on the TV this morning," she pauses and visibly swallows. "Hearing the update on the death toll in this gang war?" She rolls her eyes as she repeats what the reporter called it. Looking over her shoulder at me and then reaching for another plate, she tells me, "At least I know we're safe."

I can only nod and accept the plate. I've been 'safe' all my life. There's no such thing as safe, only the illusion of it. Telling Addison that won't help her though.

My fork shuffles the eggs around on the plate while Addison watches, but she doesn't say anything about it. I try to take a bite and then another, but it's flavorless and it only makes the pit in my stomach feel heavier.

"Are you going to read it?" she asks me and then tilts her head toward the note.

I nod once and finally reach for it, but after I read it, I don't tell her who it's from. I don't tell her what it says either.

All I know is that Eli read it and I don't know what that means for me.

ARIA,

Meet me tomorrow night. I just need to see you. I need to know you're all right.

Meet me at the candy shoppe on Main Street. You can walk there; I'll be there. I promise.

Tomorrow. Eight at night.

Yours,

Nikolai

"ARE YOU ALL RIGHT?" she asks me as I feel the blood drain from my face.

The sound of my fork abruptly scraping against the plate drowns out my answer to her. I mutter, "I just need a second," as I walk past her with the note clenched tight in my hand. It feels like a betrayal of Carter to see Nikolai. But I need to. I have to see him. I have to know he's all right.

My steps are deliberate as I walk as quickly as I can toward the stairwell, intent on searching out Eli. I don't have to look far; he's waiting for me at the top of the stairs.

"Eli," I speak his name quickly like I can't get it out fast enough. The uncertainty I'm feeling makes my skin tingle as I hold up the note.

"Aria," he says my name back easily and as if nothing's wrong.

"You read this?" I ask him even though he already told me he did.

He only nods.

"Are you going to stop me from seeing him?" I ask

him, the strength in my voice threatening to vanish at any moment.

"It depends."

"On what?" I ask him with no patience at all.

"On what Carter tells me to do," he answers, and I stand here helplessly in front of him.

"Are you going to kill him?" It's the next logical thought.

He hesitates, and I plead with him, "I won't run from you if you let me go to him. I need to see him."

He only takes a moment to respond, "I'm waiting to hear Carter's decision," and I can't contain my frustration any longer.

"You go ahead and wait. My decision is made." I know my words mean nothing to the cadre of soldiers surrounding me. It's a false threat, but I'm done playing these games where I'm some damsel trapped in a tower.

"Before you storm off," Eli begins with a straight face before I can turn my back on him and do exactly as he thought I would, storm off.

He holds out a package and I stare at it cautiously rather than take it. "What is it?" I ask him.

"You don't trust me now?" he asks with a hint of an asymmetric grin.

I don't respond. This isn't a game to me, it's my life.

"It's from Carter." He holds it out to me and I finally accept it, reeling with emotions I can't even begin to describe.

"What is it?" I ask him, but he only shrugs. The box

isn't particularly big or small, so I can't even begin to guess what it contains.

"Tell him I want to see Nikolai... please."

With a short nod, he puts his hands behind his back and takes his position as if guarding the stairwell was what he was told to do. And maybe he was. Maybe Carter thought I'd run down the stairs and out the door the moment I got a note from Nikolai.

I don't wait to get to the bedroom to open the package. I peel back the tape as I walk, and force open the box.

Inside is a phone, simple and black, and art supplies, a drawing pad, and colored pencils.

Such little things, but I stare at them on the bed for far too long in silence, wishing I hadn't grown up in this world.

CHAPTER 9

Carter

HOURS HAVE PASSED, but she hasn't moved from the bed. Occasionally she flips open the sketch pad, but she doesn't draw like she did before.

Mostly she looks at the phone, expecting it to ring.

She's waiting on me. She's waiting for my move, but I don't know what the best action to take is.

Every time my phone rings and I'm given intel on where the men are and where they're going, my orders are immediate, confident, and not to be questioned. All who stand in my way will fall.

But what Aria wants... I sit back in my seat, observing her as she stares at the pad in her lap. I don't know how much leeway to give her. Free of her cage, my songbird might very well never come back to me given what I'm planning to do. And I can't have that. Aria is mine.

"How many men did Romano send in there?" Daniel asks as he walks into the office unannounced. No knocking whatsoever. I guess some things don't change.

Taking a deep breath that stretches my back, I answer him, "Four."

"And he wants us to send a dozen?" His tone is incredulous, but I had the same exact reaction and I give him a look that says as much.

Turning my attention to Daniel, I take in his dark eyes and the rough stubble that's overgrown on his jaw. He's still in the same shirt he was wearing yesterday too.

"Did you sleep?" I ask him, and he shakes his head no, but he moves the conversation back to business matters. Back to busying himself and ending the bullshit that keeps him from having Addison back.

"Jett went down late last night to Carlisle. He said this morning that he counted at least twenty-two Talvery soldiers that come and go down the block."

"That's right inside the northern border between the two of us, not between Romano and him."

"Right," he answers me, but I didn't need him to say a damn thing, I just needed a moment to think.

"Are the rest of the areas high density like that?"

"High density?" he echoes, not understanding. He hasn't been back long and he's still catching up.

"Instead of spreading his men out, he's keeping

them heavy and clustered in one area? Or is this the only street like that?" Crossing my right ankle over my left knee, I lean back in the chair and pick up a pen to tap it against the desk as I think.

"It's like that three blocks from the divide between Romano and Talvery on the upper east side. Bedford, I think it is."

"Where are the rest of them?" I ask him. "I want a count and whereabouts of his men at all times."

"We need more eyes out if we want that intel. Jett can't move if he wants to pick them off."

"Then get them."

"Most of our men are surrounding the safe house…" For the first time since beginning this conversation, he lowers his voice to confess, "I don't want to move them."

"So, we need to take on an army with only a handful of men."

"Skilled men hired for this express purpose. Men who have been waiting for this for how long?" Daniel reminds me. Most of the men we picked up came with us for a reason. Hate is a better motivator than fear is and Talvery's made more enemies in his decades of reign than I'd like to give him credit for. As he grew older, he grew harder.

I wasn't the first boy he nearly beat to death for dealing in his territory. The others had families though, families who knew exactly who was responsible. Families who came to me, knowing we shared a common enemy.

I glance at the monitor, at my songbird who's staring at nothing and consumed by her helplessness. For a split second, I wonder if she knows everything her father did. But I already know she doesn't.

Daniel continues the conversation, hellbent on coming up with a plan. "Jett thinks we could use eight men total, two on each corner of that street and the other four on the other side to clean up that area."

"Eight men, to take on their twenty?" My voice is flat, my gaze pinned to his, but all I can see is how this will go down. How we can take out each of them.

"Romano's supposed to be sending down four in the next two days to go in, since he wants clean kills to avoid the news and having to pay off more cops. But I think we should hit them tomorrow night with the automatic assault rifles we just got from the docks."

I nod my head in agreement. Clean kills take more time, time that they'll use to react. "Why wait until tomorrow?" I ask him.

"It's Sunday," Daniel reminds me. A huff leaves me, somewhat sarcastic, somewhat pathetic. There are rules in this industry if you can call it that. No women, no children. Give peace at funerals. And leave Sundays for families. They're signs of respect and boundaries. The only reason they're kept is that sometimes enemies become allies and it's easily justified by saying that the enemy always gave respect.

I know only one man who defied the laws and my little songbird stabbed that fucker to death. Not a soul defended him. And who would when his death was justified for breaking a sacred rule?

Well, that man… and then myself. I took Aria from Talvery.

"Tomorrow night then." Daniel's eyes shine brighter with the challenge of pulling this off.

"Jett can stay where he is and take out any of Talvery's men that survive the hit. We need the police to stay back for at least eight hours. Instead of going in to see who's still breathing, we let the men try to come out to read the situation, and Jett will pick them off."

"They'll be easy to pay off. I know Officer Harold will hold them back for a grand a minute."

Daniel considers it and then offers another plan. "The alternative would be using explosives. But the street is a good location and that's a mess that'll bring too much attention."

"Hit them tomorrow night with the automatics. Pay off the cops for four hours and we'll hit the Talvery line up north as a distraction with the RDX, my explosive of choice courtesy of the shit Talvery put us through. Set off the explosives there at the same time as the hit on Carlisle Street. Let them focus on the bombings while we destroy their front line."

Daniel nods in agreement, relaxing into the chair, although his foot doesn't stop tapping on the floor, giving away his anxiety.

"Who all is there?" I ask him as my own qualms creep up on me.

"What do you mean?"

"Of Talvery's men, who...?" I pause to swallow thickly and ask my brother flat out, "Are any of them Aria's family?"

"Her cousin, Brett, comes by the bakery in the morning. It looks like their usual meet-up spot. He's been there every morning for the last three days, according to Jett. But at night, no. None of her blood. What she considers family is debatable though."

"You would think Talvery would be going out full force against Romano," I answer back instead of entertaining his thoughts on who Aria's family is.

"He was until yesterday. He moved the men to Carlisle, to our border the night after the dinner." He clarifies what night he's referring to when I give him a questioning look. "The night she killed Stephan and Romano passed the message to him. Then, yesterday, something else changed."

I close my eyes remembering that night, remembering the feeling of pride and lust I had for her growing that night she ended Stephan's life. "When it was confirmed that we had Aria."

"Yeah, that's when he moved more of his men to our side."

"So, now he's coming after us?" I can't help that I smirk, loving the challenge and the flow of adrenaline in my blood.

"There are equal numbers of men posted on the two borders. But if I were him, I'd be gunning for you."

"He knows we let her kill Stephan."

"Maybe that's why it's equal and why all his men aren't raiding our turf?"

"A man with two enemies, both pointing guns at him, who knows what he's thinking?"

Daniel's tone turns morose. "I have to tell you something you aren't going to like."

"And to think... you're interrupting this pleasant conversation ..."

"Look who's making jokes now."

"Maybe I'm learning a thing from you."

"What happened last night that led him to move more men closer to us?"

I ask my brother, "Is that what you have to tell me?" I tap the pen against the desk as I think about everything Romano told me about his plans to decimate them in only four days flat.

Daniel repositions himself and nods, but his eyes are full of worry. "Romano and Talvery know where the girls are." He visibly swallows and adds, "They followed us."

I only nod, not wanting to acknowledge that truth. "Are you sure?" I ask him, feeling the tension build in my shoulders.

"Yeah," he answers with a tired voice, the fidgeting of his foot finally halting as he asks me, "What do we do with the women?"

"If she doesn't come willingly... I want mine back in the cell when this is over with."

Daniel's expression hardens. His disappointment and anger even, are evident. I don't care what I told her, what promises I've made or how fucked a position she's put me in. I don't care about any of it. The possessiveness stirs in my blood and I struggle to contain myself, so I settle on redirecting Daniel. "What you do with yours is up to you."

"You can't do that to her." Daniel dares to tell me what I can do. "You can't lock her up and expect her not to fight back."

"You're just pissed this is affecting you and Addison, and I'm sorry for that, but I'm not letting Aria walk away from me. I won't allow it." The last sentence is barely spoken through clenched teeth as my heart rate quickens and my hands form white-knuckled fists.

"Do you want a prisoner or a partner?" Daniel's question catches me off guard.

"She'll never see me as her partner. I will always be the enemy." I speak the truth that fills me with dread. This war has to happen. I will kill her father. And she will never see me as anything but an enemy once it's done.

"Not if you treat her as a partner."

"I want someone who wants me back," I confess to him. "I want her to want me back, and that will never happen once this week is done."

"You're so blinded by hate that you don't see it," Daniel tells me as if I'm a fool.

"You and Addison are different. Don't look at me like we're in the same situation. And you fucking know that's true." He shakes his head but remains silent.

"I'll put her back in the cell if I have to," I tell him

with finality, staring past him and at the closed door. She wanted me once and I'll make it happen again. She'll learn to forgive.

"What are you doing? I've never seen you like this." Daniel's expression is worried, but more than that, sympathetic.

"I loved her," I say, and my answer is harsh; I can feel my control slipping again. It slips so easily with her.

"And?" he questions me as if he doesn't understand. As if it isn't obvious that the woman I love is the enemy. Even when all of them are dead and I've taken her back, I will always be the enemy to her and there's nothing I can do about it. Not a damn thing.

"You still love her, so why would you do that to her?"

"I don't know what love is."

"You're being fucking stupid and this 'woe is me' bullshit doesn't look good on you, Carter."

"Fuck you," I seethe as I tell my brother off. "Addison will run, and you'll follow like a little puppy dog, but she'll come back to you because you didn't do a damn thing to her. Aria..." My throat gets tighter as I speak, threatening to strangle me if I speak the words aloud. "I'm going to kill her family. I've locked her up, I've punished her."

"What you have is different, but it's obvious to her that you love her. You'll see."

"Love isn't enough sometimes. I don't know how you've gotten stuck on some fantasy, Daniel. I live in the real world, where I'm the villain. So, go ahead and tell me she'll love me after this. Keep telling yourself that too. Whatever helps you sleep."

Daniel doesn't answer. A moment passes and then another before he stands up abruptly and leaves me alone.

The second the door slams shut, I turn back to the monitors, focusing on them as my blood simmers and my gut starts to churn.

My body is ringing with anger, contempt, and fear. I haven't felt fear in so long. True fear threatens to consume me at the very real possibility of losing her.

Not if you treat her as a partner. Daniel's words echo in my head, but how can he say that when he knows what that means in this world we inhabit?

Aria's still staring at the phone and without hesitation, I pick up the phone on my desk and call her.

Only yesterday, she lay across my desk while I played with her cunt and her ass, knowing she loved it and thinking she loved me.

A day can change everything.

The line only rings once before she answers, cradling the phone close with both hands.

"Hello?" Just the sound of her voice is soothing. Everything about her is a balm for the burning rage inside of me.

"Do you hate me?" I ask her, needing to know.

"Have you killed them?"

A sad smirk kicks my lips up as I touch the tips of my fingers to the screen. I can see her swallow as the silence stretches, I can see her start to crumble when I don't immediately respond. And I hate it. I hate that this is what will happen to her.

"No." The moment I speak the word, her head falls forward and I hear her take in a deep breath. "But you know it has to happen," I remind her as she sits up straighter, still cross-legged on the bed.

"I know," she answers. I watch as she picks at the comforter and then readjusts but winces as she moves. No doubt the lashes from the belt are causing her pain. They barely left a mark on her. I held back, but even so, I know she's still hurting from it.

I struggle to breathe as she asks me, "So, it's inevitable that I'll hate you then?"

"That's your choice."

"I know some of the men who have died already," she confesses with pain etched in her voice. Her words are so strangled and unwilling to be spoken that I almost don't hear her. It takes me a second and then another, the ticks of the clock marking each of them.

She covers her mouth with her hand, pulling the phone to one side as she gathers her composure, but keeps the other end pressed close to her ear.

"There is always loss in this business," is all I can give her until I think to add, "I'm sorry."

"I'm sorry too," she tells me after a moment.

"This is no different than before when men standing in front of your father were shot, so to speak. They fight for him, and they die for him. It's all happened before."

"I'll tell you something that maybe you don't find obvious, Carter." Aria finds her strength and it gives me hope until she speaks. "I hated the men who killed them before. I just didn't have a face to associate with their deaths."

"Romano."

"What?" she questions and in even a single word, I feel the hope start to rise inside of me again.

"Direct your hate there, not at me." Maybe I'm a coward for hiding behind Romano while I can, but she can't hate me. I don't know what I'll become if she does.

She lies back slowly on the bed, ever so slowly, and stares at the ceiling before she asks, "This, wasn't you?

"I haven't had to do anything yet, but things have changed."

"What's changed?" she immediately asks, but her voice is even, devoid of emotion. I can hear her swallow as she asks me, "What exactly has changed?" She bunches the top sheet in her hand absently, waiting for my answer.

I question telling her for only a moment. But ultimately, I decide to give her what she wants. To treat her like a partner in this.

"The number of your father's men that have moved closer to Carlisle Street."

"Where's Carlisle?" she asks with her hand falling back onto the bed, but still gripping the sheet.

As much as she'd like to know what's going on, she has so much to learn.

"One street up from where our territories are divided, Miss Talvery." My cock hardens as I speak to her like this as if I'm negotiating with the enemy. My little songbird is playing the part of the queen. And what a queen she would make.

"I don't like it when you call me that," she says quietly, but her lips stay parted long after the word is spoken. I watch on the screen as her hand moves to her belly.

"Your father is preparing to invade and conquer and he's making it obvious."

"He's defending his territory." She's quick to reply, and I find her logic appropriate. Which makes me sit back farther in my seat.

"Remember who you are, Aria."

"I'm still figuring out who I am, Carter." The air of dominance wraps around her like a cloak when she talks to me like that, with only a whisper of submission. When she gives herself to me with no pretense, only honesty.

And I take that moment to tell her exactly who she is and will always be. "You're mine."

"Am I?" Her voice is coated in sadness as she closes her eyes.

"Yes," the word is practically hissed as I lean closer to the screen, wishing I were there with her now.

"And if I leave this place; if I leave… to see someone?" she asks me, and I know exactly what she's talking about. "Would I still be yours?" My pulse hammers in my ears and I bite back the initial response and the next.

I give her the only truth I know, "You will always be mine."

"Carter," Aria's voice breaks and she covers her eyes with her hand as she talks. "I'm scared."

"You're brave," I tell her, and she lets out a humorless laugh on the other end of the phone.

"I'm afraid I'm going to fail and we'll both be left with no one," she tells me, wiping under her eyes and repositioning herself on the bed, once again wincing. My gaze flicks to the nightstand where I left the cooling balm, still right where it was last night.

Ignoring her statement and refusing to think of that possibility, I ask her instead, "Are you still hurting from your punishment?"

Again, I'm given that huff of a laugh before she answers, "Yes. You left your mark on me, Mr. Cross."

"It's not the only mark I want to leave on you, songbird."

I hear her breathe in deeply on the other end and I lower my voice, forgetting everything but the two of us when I ask her, "Do you love it when I call you that?"

A second passes before she whispers, "Yes."

Again, I reach up to the screen, wishing I could touch her right now. But I can't. Not when I know the enemy could come at any moment. My men will stay with her and protect her. So long as she's safe, that's all that matters.

"You need to use the balm I gave you," I tell her and watch for her reaction.

She glances at it but doesn't move. The tension rises inside of me at her ignoring the request. A request made to help her.

"What if I want to feel it?" she asks me before I can scold her, and confusion runs through me. "What if I think I deserve to still feel the pain and I don't want the balm?" Her voice cracks slightly, but she holds her ground.

My poor Aria. The weight of two conflicting worlds is resting on her shoulders. And the consequences are heavier than any one person could possibly bear.

"You need to heal, so that if you disobey me again," I tease her, "I'll have a fresh canvas to work with when you do." I feel the ease of a smile grow on my face as the tension subsides with her genuine laughter. It's muted, soft, and just as feminine as Aria is.

"I guess I didn't think of that," she says before climbing to the edge of the bed and kicking off the thin sweatpants she's wearing. She isn't wearing any underwear.

The realization reminds me that I'm hard for her.

My dick throbs as it presses against my zipper and I want to lean back, to readjust, but I find myself leaning in closer to the monitor.

Holding the phone between her ear and her shoulder, she's able to grab the balm. She asks me, "Can you see me right now?"

"Yes."

I'm rewarded with a small smile on her lips as she looks around the room, searching for cameras she won't find.

"Put the balm down, Aria," I command her, feeling my cock twitch with need. I watch as she obeys me, setting it back down and standing in nothing but a thin cotton t-shirt.

"Yes, Carter," she simpers into the phone.

"Put the phone on speaker," I tell her, keeping my voice even so she won't have an inkling of my deep and heavy lust for her. She does as I tell her, and the moment she does I give her another command. "Set it on the bed and get on all fours like how I had you last night."

With the angle of the camera, I can see her pussy easily. I can even see up her shirt as it hangs around her waist and her pale pink nipples are obviously visible. "You're fucking perfect," I groan deep in my throat as I unzip my pants and fist my cock, pumping it once and then again.

Swallowing hard I watch as her fingers move to her sex, and she glistens with arousal.

"Do you like this, Mr. Cross?" she asks me with the sultry voice of a vixen.

"Miss Talvery, I fucking love it." I push my confession through clenched teeth. As I stroke myself, she presses her fingers into her cunt and when she does, her eyes close and her cheek pushes against the pillow.

Her lips part and I can just barely hear the sweet moan of pleasure.

"I wish I could shove my cock down your throat right now," I tell her as precum leaks from my slit. I rub it over the head of my dick and shivers of desire run down my spine and straight through my body, making my toes curl.

Like the good girl she is, she tells me back, "You'd make me choke on it. I love it when you do that." Her dirty words make my cock impossibly hard and I know I'm going to cum.

"Fuck yourself faster," I command her, and she immediately obeys. Pushing her small fingers in and out of her tight cunt. Her back bows and her hips sway with her impending orgasm.

"Hold still and grab your ass where I struck you while you cum for me," I tell her as my balls draw up. And she does. With her head pressed into the pillow, one hand squeezing the marks on her ass and the other fucking herself, she cums violently, falling to her side and screaming out my name.

My name.

I lose myself with her, cumming into my hand like a high school prick and wishing there was nothing that separated us. Wishing we lived in a different world.

CHAPTER 10

Aria

It's an odd rush of emotion that flows through me. The fear and anxiety are most easily described, but there are others tangled in a knot in the pit of my stomach.

Carter made it all go away when he told me to touch myself. Submitting to him makes everything go away and the feeling lasts long after he hangs up the phone.

As I walk out of the bedroom, knowing I'm doing something he'd prefer I didn't, the haze and comfort that comes from submitting to him dims. It's a consequence I accept. Before he ended our conversation, he told me what I chose tonight is up to me. He's giving me the choice, and I won't waste it.

I want to be more than I have been all my life.

A touch of shame washes over me as I think, *I want to be a woman who could stand by Carter's side.* It's shameful because this isn't for Carter. This meeting isn't for my father.

This meeting with Nikolai isn't even for him.

It's for me.

My heart pounds in my chest, as does the adrenaline in my blood. Tonight, I'll live up to my name. To be Aria Talvery, daughter of a ruthless crime lord. And a woman standing between two men waging war.

My father would have me stay willingly in my room. My lover would have me stay willingly locked in his house.

I'll stay and stand where I want after tonight until I see my end. No matter if that means I'll lose both men.

Even if the pleasure Carter gave me only an hour ago is still coursing through my veins.

I can hear Addison making something in the kitchen and I hesitate to go in to see her. I haven't told her a damn thing and it feels like I'm lying to her by keeping these secrets from her.

As I step in to tell her I'm going out, the microwave beeps and the smell of chicken noodle soup fills my lungs. Comfort food, even though there's no comfort here.

The air is easy between us, but I know it won't last when she turns around and sees me. I've been struggling with whether or not I should tell her since I got the note. I want to lean on her, to confide in her, but I also want to save her from this awfulness that rages inside of me.

I don't know what to do. I honestly have no idea what to do, but I know if she asks me, I'll tell her about everything. And I'll never lie to her.

"Dinner?" I ask her as she pulls the door open, not peeking back behind her to answer me. I wish she would. I wish I could get this part over with.

"You want some?" she asks softly, devoid of the cheeriness I anticipate from her. I watch as she sets the bowl down after removing the paper towel covering the top and trashing it. That's when she finally looks up at me.

"Are you okay?" I ask her a question first, but she ignores it, asking her own instead.

"Where are you going?" Addison's voice is thick with sleep. "Are you meeting Carter?" The deep crease in the center of her forehead is evidence enough of her concern, but she quickly fists her hands and places one on each hip as her chest rises. The act actually makes me smile and eases some of the nerves bubbling inside of my chest.

I love her and her protectiveness. I wish I could hide in it.

"I have a meeting with someone else," I tell her and feel that unease rise up higher, into my throat and bringing true fear with it as she asks me, "Does Carter know?"

"Yes," I answer her in a single unsteady breath.

Shifting her weight from one foot to the other, she

doesn't respond, and I watch as the fight in her subsides. I can read the questions on her face, but she chooses not to ask any of them. The biggest two being "who?" and "why?" I was so like her once in my life.

"I'll be okay." I can at least give her that to ease her worries, although it feels like I won't be okay. It feels like I'm risking everything, and the consequences will be severe. I know it all already, I've weighed all the risks and thought of each outcome.

But I have to do this. "I have to try something to stop all of this." I give her a little more, hinting at what I'm doing, but she doesn't ask additional questions.

"You surprise me," Addison admits, her lips turned down into a frown although I'm not sure why.

"What's wrong?" I ask, ignoring the obvious and feeling my heart try to climb into my throat. I cautiously step closer, not wanting to hurt her or leave her feeling like she's anything but my friend, my closest friend.

I have to clasp my hands together in front of me to keep from reaching out to her, but it doesn't matter, because she reaches out to me first. Brushing her hand against my forearm, she gives me a hesitant smile.

"You handle it all so much better than I do, and I just..." As she trails off, her tone says it all. *She feels weak.*

I can't stand her reaction and I squash her thoughts as quickly as I can. "I don't handle it well; I barely handle it at all." I try to joke with her, but it doesn't work. She takes in a deep, unsteady breath and then looks back to the bowl of soup.

"Daniel asked me to forgive him yesterday."

The sudden change in topic startles me and I don't know if she's upset with me or not. I ask in a near whisper, "What did you say?"

"I said that I didn't know how I could. That when I fell in love with him, he was a different man."

"I'm sorry," I tell her as I grab her hand.

She's choked up and I find it contagious as she looks up toward the tallest cabinet and speaks to it, rather than me to keep from crying. "He said I'm good at lying to myself but that it's okay and that he still loves me." She sniffles, wiping under her eyes even though the tears haven't fallen yet. "Can you believe the balls he has?" Her lips twitch up into a sad smirk, but it doesn't stay long as she gives in to the tears.

"I miss him," she cries softly into my shoulder and clings to me. I'm quick to hold her tightly, hugging her as she breaks down. It fucking hurts seeing her like this. If I could go back, I'd keep her from learning the truth. I wish she'd never seen what happened. I wish she'd never peeked into this world I can't escape.

She pulls away after only a few seconds, shaking out her hands and walking away, but then comes right back. Her unease shows as she paces like I do but in much smaller circles.

"I feel crazy," she mutters and sniffles again.

"The Cross boys are good at making the women they love go crazy," I answer her in a deadpan tone with a weak smile. It takes a minute for her to look me in the eyes, and when she does, she doesn't accept the humor in my response.

"I swear I didn't know the things they do. But he told me he's always been a bad man and that it never stopped him from loving me. Or me from loving him before."

I rub her arm, feeling like it's all my fault and hating myself for it. I wish I could go back. If only I could. There's so much I would change.

"I want to leave with him, but he won't leave his brothers and I don't think I could ever ask him to do that, but together they will live like this... rule like this."

"He's not a bad man, Addie." I don't know where she's going with this, but I refuse to let her focus on something that will never change. "And what they do... they do because they have to." I swallow down the pain of the words, knowing I've had to choke on that excuse for as long as I've lived.

"How can we live like this, knowing what they do? What they're capable of?"

"We remember why they are the way they are. And we give them the love they need, so long as they give it back to us." I stare into her eyes, meaning every word.

"I know they need love. They desperately need to be loved." Tears prick at my own eyes as she looks away from me, but I see from her expression that she knows it's true. There's nothing in the world that would deny that truth.

Addison wipes under her eyes with the sleeves of

her pajama shirt. She's dressed for bed, exhausted and dealing with the weight of loving a man from the world I grew up in. Part of me is jealous of her, a very small part, but it's there. "He loves you, Addie," I whisper to her, squeezing her hand.

She squeezes mine back and then lets her hand drop to her side. "I know, but if I accept it, I'm no better than he is. And I'll never be okay with what Carter did to you. I don't care if you are."

"Carter and Daniel are different men." My answer comes out harsher than I wanted, and I attempt to soften it by adding, "And I know Carter's reason, Addie." I try to tell her more, but the words won't come out. I can't tell her about what my father did and what Carter thinks he heard. If I told her that, the next logical thing to say would be that it wasn't me he heard. The voice he heard that gave him the strength to keep living didn't belong to me.

My heart plummets painfully in my chest at the thought of my secret, making me feel sick once again.

"When are you leaving me?" Addie asks, changing the subject again and moving back to the counter to grab a spoon from the drawer. The metal clinks against the ceramic as she stirs her soup. "A secret meeting in the middle of the night?" She tries to add a sense of playfulness into the chide, but it doesn't come out strong enough.

As I answer her, she lifts the spoon to her lips, blowing on the soup and then swallowing it.

"Not so secret, and I'll be back soon."

"Should I ask what it's about?"

I don't know what to tell her, and I remember all the times I was curious but too afraid to ask. I wish someone had taken my fear away from me and told me more about the world I was living in. That's what fuels me to tell her, "I'm meeting a friend I grew up with who's one of my father's men."

Her face pales as she peeks toward the doorway to the kitchen. Maybe she expects to find Eli there, I don't know, but then she whispers, "Should you be doing that?"

Her eyes plead with me to be truthful and so I answer her honestly, putting a hand on her shoulder and not daring to take my gaze away from hers as I say, "I should have done it sooner."

"What if he tries to take you back?" The raw note of fear in her voice means more to me than I could ever tell her.

I shake my head. "Eli is coming with me, and Carter knows about it. I'm not leaving you, Addison. I promise. He wouldn't let it happen."

"So, you two…?" She doesn't finish the question.

"Are… speaking, but still not okay," I answer slowly.

"Why go then?" she asks, and I know she'll understand my reasoning.

"He's my friend, and he's going to die or he's going to help kill the man I love." Tears brim, but I hold them back. It's the painful truth, and I know I need to change it. "If I don't do something, those are the only two outcomes."

"Are you..." Addie looks anywhere but at me, until she gathers her thoughts and finally asks a question I don't know the answer to. "Whatever you tell him, or ask of him... will he listen to you?"

Cason comes into view from the very doorway she was just looking toward. "I don't know," I answer her with a weak smile, although I stare back at Cason. Something thuds hard within my chest knowing Nikolai has always tried to keep things from me. He thinks it protects me, but I know now that he's wrong.

Addison's gaze follows mine and the clinking of her spoon against the bowl as she places her dishes in the sink marks the finality of our discussion. "Be safe," she tells me quietly as she leaves.

"You too," I tell her and listen to the sound of her retreating down the hall to the bedrooms as Cason steps into the kitchen. His jeans are dirty, covered in mud from the knees down.

He was doing something... and I can only imagine it involved a shovel and shallow grave.

"I heard you might be going out." Cason starts talking the moment Addie's out of the kitchen. I wonder if she stopped in the hall, holding her breath and staying as still as she can so she can listen.

I've done that more times than I can count.

"I am." My answer is hard as I look Cason in the eye. "Right now, actually."

"Are you sure you want to do that?" he questions me. The man's nearly a foot taller than me, with broad shoulders and arms that are a dead giveaway he spends too much time in the gym.

"You're the muscle." I ignore his question and ask him my own. "Aren't you?"

He tilts his head, considering me.

"You guys have a certain look to you," I explain as I walk through the kitchen and head to the living room. It's a modern house with an open concept floor plan, so he has no problem viewing me as he crosses his arms and leans against the wall.

"The scar on your chin, the tattoos across your knuckles, probably where they're scarred too," I speak to him as the vision of men my father referred to as the muscle, invades my memory. They'd come to the house every once in a while, with big envelopes stuffed full of cash they'd leave for him. As polite as they were to me, I knew what they did.

They beat the shit out of men who didn't pay up. My gaze drifts to the mud on Cason's shins... and they buried the men who didn't learn the lesson fast enough.

Slipping on my shoes, leather ballet flats, I peek up at Cason and ask him, "Do you have bullet hole scars too?"

His eyes are still assessing me as the silence drags on. It doesn't even look like he's breathing as I stand tall and make my way back to him. There's a matte black earpiece in his right ear, and I wonder if Carter's listening. I wonder if Carter's asking him to stop me because he doesn't have the balls to do it himself.

Fed up with Cason forcing me to talk to myself, I tell him, "It's three blocks down, and Eli is accompanying me. Thank you for your concern."

As I walk toward the stairway, glancing at the clock on the stove to make sure I'm on schedule, Cason decides to walk in front of me, his large chest becoming as unyielding and firm as a brick wall.

"I urge you to reconsider," he tells me with a voice that comes from deep in his throat. Towering over me, he's a man who creates fear. And it stirs in my blood, warning me to back down and simply survive the encounter. I look him in the eyes and tell him calmly with a hint of a smile and a narrowed glare, "See, I knew you were the muscle." Inwardly, I feel like I'm about to choke on a spiked ball of panic.

I stare into his dark eyes, meeting his gaze and refusing to back down. Not this second, and not the next. Never.

"I'm going," I tell him with finality and strength I don't feel anywhere else.

"As you wish." His answer is accompanied by a look of disappointment. Clenching his jaw, he moves his gaze back to the kitchen.

My body sags and I heave in a breath when Cason turns his back to me to go down the stairs first. The sinking feeling that chills every inch of my skin is something I've felt before and I hate it. It will always come. Those who are bigger, scarier, and hold an air of darkness around them will always bring out my survival instinct to run. But they die just like the rest of us.

I only peek up to Cason's back when I hear him as he grabs his ear. I can hear the bellowing that's coming from it from where I stand.

"Aria," Cason starts speaking before he's fully turned to me. "Please forgive me for trying to intimidate you." He chokes on his words as if terrified of getting them wrong and the look in his eyes couldn't be further from the look that gave me goosebumps only moments ago.

"I forgive you," I answer him slowly, questioning my own response and wanting to know what the fuck just happened. The question lingers in my words as they reach his ear. Or rather, the earpiece that's still filled with the yells of someone on the other end. An enraged Carter, naturally. My lips threaten to tug into a smile as I hear his voice, but I contain it as Cason continues.

"Your decisions are your own and I have absolutely no right to interfere. I'm only here to protect you."

It's as if he's speaking an oath. His gaze is genuinely full of remorse and I wonder what he really thinks of me. I haven't thought of that at all until this moment.

"I'll never turn my back on you again," he tells me with both of his hands clasped in front of him apologetically. He even lowers his head some, hunching his shoulders to meet my gaze at eye level. "Would you like me to take you to Eli?"

"No need." Eli's voice startles me and I'm ashamed I jump backward. Eli's smile is wicked like he's proud he got to me. With my hand on my chest and my back against the wall, he passes me a white jean jacket.

"You scared me," I tell him in the same breath I exhale. My heart still feels like it's about to leap out of my chest.

"I know," he says, grinning like a Cheshire cat before resuming his normal dominating stance.

"Carter wanted me to give this to you, in case you'd be needing it," he tells me, and I snatch it from him. It matches my outfit, which I do and don't like about this situation. I want to ask where the cameras are. I want to question both men and demand they tell me everything Carter tells them, but I don't want to give away how little I know. Not to them.

"Asshole," I mutter as I right myself and steady my breath. Cason lets out a snort of a laugh and the tension between the three of us eases some. But only for a moment.

"I'm sorry, Aria," Cason tells me as I drape the jacket over my forearm. "I have strong opinions and I know I need to keep them to myself and I'm sorry," he rambles slightly, but his tone is genuine, and his green eyes shine with remorse.

"I get it," I tell him. "I know what war means and what this means." I look him in the eyes as I answer and neither of us wavers, not until Eli speaks up.

"Are you ready to meet with the enemy?" Eli asks

me, and I can't look at either of them as I answer, "I already have."

From the corner of my eye, I see the smile wane on his face, but Eli nudges me with his shoulder before walking out in front.

"Be smart, Aria," Cason warns as my small footsteps echo in the foyer. My quickened pulse increases even more and I have to walk a little quicker to keep up with Eli.

It didn't feel real until just now.

The crickets are out tonight, and the sky is lit with so many stars. More stars than I've ever seen in Fallbrook.

"How long until we're there?" I ask Eli, breathing in the crisp air of the cool summer night and ignoring the roiling in the pit of my stomach. The anxiety numbs my hands and I clench and unclench them before deciding to shrug on the jacket and slip my hands into my pockets.

Taking a look around to my left and right, this street is nothing but houses. I barely remember that from the drive up. The next street is where the houses are grouped closer together and there's something on the corner, a church or a liquor store, maybe both. I don't remember.

"Not long, he's already waiting," Eli tells me, but the playfulness, the easiness from the stairwell are all but forgotten.

He glances at me as I keep my pace steady with his, taking strides more often since he's taller than me. The sound of a car driving up the next street over makes him pause and he holds his arm out, stopping me from moving out into the street and pushing me closer to the brick fence of the house to my left. A moment passes, and the sound of the car diminishes. The voices from the same earpiece Cason was wearing make me stare at Eli. I can't hear what they're saying, but I know he's getting information about something.

Dread and panic mix together, making my legs feel weak. Eli glances up at the house, to the second floor and waits, then a sound creeps into his ear and he nods.

The nod wasn't for me and as Eli looks down at me and smiles politely, both of us know it.

"It's clear, Miss..." He stops and clears his throat then says, "Aria."

The dread's still there, making my hands clammy and causing my throat to tighten.

"I was hoping you wouldn't do this," Eli tells me and continues to stare straight ahead even as I look up at him, willing him to look me in the eyes.

Since he doesn't look back at me, I stare straight ahead as well. "If you thought I'd lie down and let this go on without trying to stop it, you were wrong."

"There's no way to stop this."

"I stood by before and did nothing while I watched family die," I speak quietly and swallow the knot that forms in my throat as I think of my mother. After taking a moment to compose myself, I tell Eli with finality, "I won't do it again."

CHAPTER 11

Carter

I HATE BEING in this office. Watching cameras and waiting. I don't miss the rush of being on the streets, but I hate not being beside the men who are risking their lives for me right now. Without the first move made on this side, the leaks and intel can't be trusted.

I'm waiting. The adrenaline competes inside of me with the hate and pent-up rage. And here I sit. Waiting.

"Carter." Jace's voice carries through the closed door. I haven't left since Daniel slammed it shut earlier and it's only now that I remember our fight. My brothers rotate in and out of my office, I'm used to them coming and going. And seemingly forgetting past conversations in order to handle business.

"Come in," I call out to him, and instantly the door opens.

"The Red Room, the stash in the backroom is gone, and the fucker who broke in last night to take it was found face down in the river this morning." Jace's words come out like an assault as he paces to the chair across from me, gripping the back of it and staring at me waiting for answers.

All day, this is what I do. Accept information and move chess pieces. That's how true empires are built. The bloodshed is nearly the conquering of a knight. Some poor fool dies, so the men with power make a simple move, knowing more are to come and there's more game left to play.

"Do the cops have any idea who did it?" I ask him, bringing my thumb to my chin and running the pad along the stubble there. I need to shave. Jace and I are more alike than I care to admit. The back and forth of the motion keeps me focused on Jase and this shitstorm.

Jace speaks in rapid fire, giving me all the details from his conversation with Officer Harold. No leads on a suspect, no trace of him on any city cameras once he leaves the edge of town and heads down to the woods on the edge of Jersey. Yet, he's found dead at the river next to his house hours later.

"It doesn't add up," I answer Jace, meeting his gaze as he lowers himself to the chair opposite mine on the other side of my desk. His thumb raps on the armrest as he nods.

"Someone's fucking with us. Letting us know that they can steal from us, kill on our turf, and they can get away with it."

"Marcus," I say the name without thinking. "He's the only man who's ever been able to get away with that shit."

"And only because he's a fucking ghost with no face." He takes a calming breath before adding, "Just one look on a tape and we've got his ass."

"How many decades now has he gotten away with it? Any territory, any head he wants severed?"

"Why fuck with us though? Why us?" He leans forward, letting the anger show in his voice and his posture.

"Daniel turned on him first, blaming him for what happened to Addison with no proof." Instead of indulging in the rage of having product stolen from us and the opportunity for justice torn from my hands, I consider everything logically. It's how it needs to be handled. With nothing but cold-hearted control.

"I don't know... If he set up Addison..." Jase's thoughts are left unfinished, but I know what he's thinking. If Marcus is after us, it's only a matter of time before we find out what he truly wants.

And if he went after Addison, he won't stop until he has her.

"The cameras and men have the safe house fully under surveillance?" I question Jase, although it's more of a reminder to myself. He nods with his thumb brushing across his lip.

"Yeah, there's no way he'd get in without us knowing."

"And who knows?" I ask him as the pieces fall one by one into the puzzle of how to handle this.

"Who knows what?" he asks to clarify, a brow lifting.

"Who knows we had someone steal from us and then they turned up dead?"

"Jared and two of his men. The men in our pocket at the station want to know what to do; they haven't asked outright, but they think it was our hit on the fucker."

"Good." My quick response in a hardened voice surprises my brother. He should know better by now. "Tell Jared I handled the prick who broke in. Tell the police that we're grateful for their cooperation and pay them off." Jase's eyes go wide and a look of outrage is there for only a moment. But as soon as it comes, it's gone.

"So, no one thinks we don't have this under control?" he surmises.

"Exactly."

"But we don't."

"It's about perception, Jase. One moment of what could look like weakness and our allies become enemies. The men we have under our thumb think they can wiggle free and take a shot back."

"What do I do about finding out who did this shit?"

"Put Declan on it. He needs to go through home security system footage around the river starting at the dead fuck's house. We can't rely on the city surveillance."

As Jase nods, he settles into the chair. No one steals from us or fucks with us. Even Marcus wouldn't dare. I never thought it was him when it came to Addison. Daniel came up with that shit himself because he had no one else to blame.

"I'll let Declan know," he tells me, still nodding in agreement.

"You're not going to tell me one thing and then turn around and tell our men something else, are you?" I let the words slip out with my disappointment and a trace of animosity evident in my tone.

"Don't do that shit," he bites back, shaking his head. "Tell me I didn't do the right thing, and I'll apologize."

The large clock ticks steadily in the background as my grip tightens on the armrest and a tic in my jaw spasms.

"You were... in a state where I think you would agree I needed to step in." He raises his hands quickly as my gaze narrows and the temperature of my blood rises. "It was a difficult night, and I would have never stepped in if what happened wasn't *exactly* how it happened."

My blunt nails dig into the leather armrests as I try to contain my anger, even as my brother sits there as if we're just having a casual conversation as if he's no threat to me.

"I won't do it again," he tells me easily, and then clears his throat. "I didn't want..." he trails off and looks away over to his left, to the box still on the ground and out of place. "I just," he looks back up at me and I can read the sincerity on his face, "I didn't want her to hate you."

It takes a moment for him to contain the uncertainty and pain in his expression. With each second, every tick of the clock, the truth of what he says chips away at the resentment I feel over what he did. "You've been mad at me before; I know you'll get over it. This isn't the first time I've crossed the line and it won't be the last. But I love you, as my brother and my friend, and I didn't want her to hate you. I know you love her."

I haven't seen Jase like this in years. Not since the last funeral he went to. And the second his confession is over, he starts up a new conversation, never giving me the chance to respond.

"I didn't come in here to bother you with this shit."

My throat is dry, and I reach behind me for two tumblers and whiskey before asking him, "What shit did you come in to bother me with then?"

"About Aria meeting with Nikolai."

"I know she decided to go. I spoke to Eli when they left."

"She already left?" he questions, shaking his head. "What is he going to tell her?"

"It doesn't matter," I say to put an end to his bullshit. "I let her go. She wanted to go to him." I down the whiskey in my glass before pouring myself more and then pouring three fingers into his glass and offering it to him.

He takes it but doesn't drink.

"How many men did he bring?" he asks me.

"Just him," I tell him, and he lets a smirk spread on his face in response.

"He may be young, but even I'm not that stupid."

"I know why he did it." Even though I realize I'm talking to Jase, I speak absently, knowing why Nikolai came alone and what he bargained away just for her to get the note. "He's desperate."

"He has a death wish," Jase speaks up, and I move my attention from him to the screen.

"I told Eli to let her make the decision. If she wants to go to him, let her... and she did."

"It would be easy to simply lock the door and coming from me..." Jase shakes his head and takes the first sip of his whiskey.

"I want to see what she'll do." Every ounce of me wants to control her. To demand she behave exactly how I want her to. Even as I stared at the monitor a half hour ago on the computer, watching her as she picked up a silk blouse I bought her, intending on wearing it for him, the urge to get to her faster than she could walk into that room raced through my mind. To keep her there if I couldn't convince her otherwise.

"Are you sure that you're sure?" Jase questions me again. I should feel angry that it's becoming a habit for him to question me, but I know he's thinking what I'm thinking, that she'll choose him again.

With a painful thud in my chest that numbs my body, I answer him, "Yes. She's already there, waiting."

"Waiting for what?"

"For me to tell Eli to let her in."

"You aren't going to be there?" he questions me with a look of complete disbelief.

Placing my palms on the desk and leaning forward so he can understand exactly why I'm not there, I ask him, "Do you think it would be helpful if he were in my presence right now?" My jaw hardens, and I can't help it as I tell him, "This is for her." It fucking hurts to admit, "She wouldn't want me there." He's shaking his head, and I shrug.

I tell Jase, "She's not in danger. The only thing that could happen is if she…"

"If she chooses him and tries to run." Jase finishes my thoughts and I nod once, bringing my attention back to the monitors. Jase looks like he's contemplating what to say next, so I remain silent.

"Eli will kill him if he tries?" I nod again at his question and throw back my second glass of whiskey.

"I just have to give Eli the go-ahead to let her in," I admit to him as I stare at the screen knowing I'm giving her what she wants, but not knowing how it will affect us and I can't fucking stand it.

The moment he touches her, I'll see her reaction.

I will never forgive her if she chooses him over me.

CHAPTER 12

Aria

I REMEMBER the first time I saw Nikolai. We were only children. His father worked for my father until he was killed.

The funeral home always had the prettiest flowers, and that's what I looked at whenever we went there, all of the pretty flowers. But that day, I let myself watch the boy next to the casket.

I never liked to look at the people there. They always cried, and it made me want to cry, but I wasn't allowed. We were Talverys and we weren't allowed to cry, no matter how much I wanted to.

The boy was crying. He was taller than me and in a black suit that didn't fit right, because he was too tall for it. His ankles were bare although his black shoes were new.

He looked so angry as he stared at the casket, wiping away his tears like they were nothing but a nuisance.

I never wanted to speak to anyone, not like my mother and father did. I never wanted to give anyone a hug or even be near any of them. Especially, the ones who smiled and laughed at funerals. I didn't understand it and it made me angry to see people laughing when they were supposed to be mourning. I didn't learn until years later that everyone mourns differently. Apparently, my coping mechanism is solitude.

And Nikolai's was anger.

I remember how hesitant I was to touch his shoulder and ask him, "Are you okay?"

He was the first person I'd ever talked to at the many funerals I'd attended by this point. When he looked at me, when he glanced over his shoulder to answer me, he had a look of pure rage, maybe even disgust, but then he saw me, and it softened. Not just softened; his expression crumpled. The boy bared his soul to me and I saw the pain and the loneliness. He didn't speak; he only shook his head. But then I tried to hug him, and he let me.

My father hired him to do collections, even though he was only fourteen. He said the boy needed a distraction and I was happy I got to see him every week.

And then my mother died. And I felt the grief, the solitude that begged me to hide away and isolate myself. But Nikolai refused to let me be alone. He promised me he'd stay with me. He was the first person who said it was okay to cry and he held me while I did.

Ever since that day, we were inseparable.

He was my only friend. My only lover. And the only person I ever trusted in this world other than my mother.

The door to the back room of a candy shop three blocks north of the safe house is all that stands between Nikolai and me. My fingers keep pinching and twisting the cuffs of the jean jacket. Deep inside of me, the fear that they've hurt Nikolai is very real. That he's cuffed to a chair and on death's door is likely. I've seen it before. So many times.

"He's okay, right?" I ask quietly, not hiding my fear as I peek up at Eli. He considers me for a long moment before nodding his head and each fraction of a second that passes ramps up my anxiety.

"Thank you," I whisper my gratitude, although I'm not sure I entirely believe him and look toward the door with my shoulders squared as if it'll open any second.

"You can go in now," Eli tells me from behind and I reach for the knob, but he stops me, gripping my forearm and telling me, "Let me."

Nodding, I wait with bated breath for the door to open. It's on rusted hinges and they screech with the motion of the heavy door opening.

"Aria," Nik breathes my name before I even see him, and his voice is drowned out by the sound of metal chair legs scraping against the concrete floor as he pushes away from a small card table in the center of the barren room. Barely aware that Eli is watching and that there are two other men in the room also watching, I run to him, meeting him halfway and clinging to him.

I don't care in this moment. They can all watch and judge.

All I can see as I hold him is the gun touching the back of his head and I can't get it out of my mind. Burying my face into his hard chest, I feel so much relief, unjustified relief, but it's there.

Nikolai holds me even tighter. Like if he loosens his grip on me, I'll be gone forever.

I inhale a deep, steadying breath as he whispers, "Thank God."

"Nik," I barely breathe his name as try to hold on to my composure. "Nik." I keep saying his name, but I can't help it. *He's okay*, I tell myself over and over as he pulls back slightly to look at me before hugging me back against his chest.

"I've missed you so much," he whispers against my hair, and I can feel his warm breath all the way down to my shoulder.

"How did you find me?" I ask him and pull back to look at him. The sight of his face shreds my composure. Faint bruises and a split lip are evidence left behind from days ago.

It's only then that he releases me, looking between me and Eli and then to the table. "Sit with me?" he asks as if there's any chance at all I would deny him, and it's the first time I can smile. It's a sad smile, the kind that comes with a pain that everyone else can feel.

"Of course," I barely get the words out and I have to clear my throat. Brushing my hair back and breathing in deeply to steady myself, I tell him, "I'm so happy to see you." My next words come out rushed. "I'm happy you're okay."

"Me too," he replies, but his voice is cloaked in sadness and he doesn't stop looking over every inch of me. "Are you okay?" he asks me and then reaches across the table to take my hand. His is large and warm, easily dwarfing my hand. Hands that have held mine for as long as I can remember.

I nod, swallowing the knot in my throat and not wanting to tell him or anyone else everything that's happened. "How did you find me?" I repeat my question and try to remember everything I wanted to tell him.

"I did what I had to do." His answer is short, but he doesn't stop rubbing soothing circles on the palm of my hand. It comforts me like he'll never know. He's done the same thing all my life. Every tragedy, every heartache. It's such a simple thing, but with that gentle touch, I can breathe, feeling as if everything is all right, even when I know it's not.

"Does my father know?"

"Yes, he…" Nik's voice gets tighter as he swallows whatever he was going to say. "He knows."

"What is it?" I ask him, and I don't hide the urgency in my voice when I demand, "Tell me everything."

"We have eyes on Carter. And I know," he struggles to keep a straight face, his fortitude failing him. "I know what he did to you," Nik says with a sickness at the end of words. "I'm so sorry, Aria." He breaks down in front of me, covering his eyes for a moment and apologizing over and over.

"Stop it." My command comes out harsher than I planned and I nearly rip my hand away from him. I won't be a charity case for sympathy.

"I swear I'll kill him." His expression hardens, and his eyes turn sharp. "I'll make him pay for what he did to you." I can see Eli shift his weight out of the corner of my eye and my pulse quickens, pounding at my temples, the adrenaline pumping harder and harder.

"No, you won't," I tell him quietly, grabbing his hand with both of mine. I hope he can read the message in my eyes telling him to shut the fuck up. Nik is hotheaded and reckless, but he can't be so stupid as to say that kind of thing right now. "Stop it," I warn him.

"After what he did to you?" he questions me, his brow furrowed, and forehead creased.

"You don't know what he did." It's all I can tell him, wanting to deny any of the accusations he could throw at me, even if they're true.

I know my expression is a mix of worry and sadness, but I can't help it. I can't control the emotions on my face. Not with Nikolai.

"I know enough. I'm going to kill him for it," Nik repeats his threat, the anger coming in full force and I feel lightheaded with indignation.

"I'll never forgive you," I whisper the words, feeling the ache sit against my ribcage, etching into my bone and eating away at whatever soul I have left.

"What's wrong with you?" Nik raises his voice with incredulity and backs away from me, his hands pushing against the edge of the flimsy table and inching it closer to me. He's breathing heavily as his composure crumbles. "He'll pay for what he did!"

"I didn't come here to talk about that," I say and struggle to look Nik in the eye. Belatedly, I remember what Carter told me about the men on Carlisle and what I'd planned to say.

"We're family," Nik reminds me, his tone wretched, his gaze covering every inch of my face and doesn't stay steady in the least. He's losing it. "I'll protect you!" he declares, and I take this moment to gain control of the conversation.

"Then move the men on Carlisle," I tell him quickly, staring into his eyes, although my words stumble into one another. Moving my hands into my lap, I resist the urge to fidget and straighten my back. "The war is between my father and Romano. Romano's the one who took me."

Nik's expression is pained as he says, "This isn't a negotiation, Aria."

He looks over at Eli, but only for a moment before giving in and spilling the plans my father has set in motion. He barely considers withholding the information and something doesn't feel right about it.

"The men on Romano's turf are decoys. He's letting them die and preparing to rampage Cross's territory."

I worry my bottom lip between my teeth and I struggle to breathe, but somehow manage to tell him, "Change his mind."

"Not after what Cross did to you."

I wish he could understand. I wish he felt like I do. I cannot fail. I won't live to see the men I love kill each other. I won't fucking do it!

"Then create a reason. Have Mika go up to... to..." I'm blanking on the street name that divides the territories. I've heard them all so many times before, but I rarely left the house. When I did, I never wandered far and so the street names mean nothing to me.

Whipping my gaze to Eli, I raise my voice and say, "Help me!" I stare at him as if he's failing me because he is. They're all failing me, and this is a losing cause. "The street where Romano territory meets Talvery territory."

"Bedford." Eli's response comes easily. He's not shaken in the least and I gather my composure, pushing my hair out of my face and staring at the steel table until I'm able to speak calmly.

"Bedford, move them up to Bedford," I plead with Nik, keeping the cadence of my voice soft and even. "Please," I beg him, desperate for him to understand.

"You think that will stop this war between Talvery and Cross?'" he asks me with an air of ridicule. "The men you're dealing with aren't men who have mercy, Aria." Nikolai talks to me as if I don't know them and it pisses me off.

I know firsthand how cruel they are.

"I'm not asking for mercy, Nik. I'm asking for fucking common sense." I practically spit the last few words. I lean back in the chair, keeping one wrist balanced on the edge of the table. "If they die, it's because you failed."

"Failed at what?" he asks me. "Taking charge of an army I don't control?"

"We have control. It's easy to take control," I say words my father once said to me. He said I needed to be harder, that I needed to wield my name and authority. I never imagined I would heed his advice.

"Send Mika to Bedford; he's at the top of the chain like you. No one would be surprised if he dies there, so make sure he does, Nikolai," I harden my voice, remembering my absolute hatred for Mika and all the evil shit he's done. "You know he deserves far less than an honorable death. Take him up there on a false pretense, shoot him in the back of the head and be done with him." I'm nearly shaken by the venom in my tone, by how meticulously I'm planning murder and interfering with war. "Tell my father it was Romano, and that you have to retaliate. Do it tonight."

"Mika's dead." It takes a moment to even comprehend what Nikolai said before he adds, "Your father killed him."

A cocktail of incredulity and anguish mix in my

blood. "What? What happened?" My questions leave me in a single breath, a quiet one as I'm too afraid to speak any louder. As if doing so would change the truth of what happened.

Nikolai glances at Eli before leaning forward and speaking in a hushed voice. "Your father thought you ran away or that you were dead. He went through the tapes and Mika was the last person to speak to you."

With a deep breath, his eyes drift from me to Eli again before he turns his attention back to me. "He asked Mika why he was there and what he said that got you so upset."

"And?" I question him, my voice not nearly as low as Nik's, but it doesn't matter. I know Eli can hear. I know they can all hear.

"Mika didn't answer fast enough. Your father shot him in the head in front of everyone."

"Oh, my God." My heart pumps the blood coldly through my veins as I picture the scene and worry about what my father is thinking and everything he's been through.

"I won't lose sleep over Mika, but your father's losing it, Aria."

My chest feels like it's collapsing, and I struggle to grab hold of every bit of anger I've had toward my father since I've been here.

"He didn't come for me." I can barely speak the words.

"As soon as he found out where you were, he did. *We* did."

A moment passes and then another. I've held so much pain and anger inside of me at the thought that my father didn't care. Fuck. I wish I knew more. I'm losing this game. Each pawn I think I can capture has already been taken before I make my first move.

"He won't move those men or hold back against Cross, Aria. He wants justice." He adds firmly and with a conviction that sends a shiver down my spine, "We all do."

"This isn't justice. It's senseless death." I stare into Nik's eyes, willing him to understand me.

"You deserve justice, Aria."

"I'm fine, Nikolai. Carter didn't do anything to me that I didn't want."

Disbelief mars his handsome features. "You aren't thinking right," he says and slowly a look of sympathy replaces any hint of anger. "Aria, please come with me."

"I can't let that happen." Eli's quick to step closer to us, and I'm equally as quick to shove my hand against his stomach and tell him to back off. Eli takes in my expression before nodding his head and falling back into place. I don't know what he saw on my face at that moment, but he'll never know how much I needed him to side with me.

"I'm not leaving, Nik, and you need to find a way to move the men. Find a way," I implore him, but not a word is getting through to him.

"I won't let you stay here," Nikolai says then puts both fists on the table, breathing heavier and looking at Eli.

"I won't let you do this; I won't let you choose to stay with a man who hurt you."

"It's my choice." I don't defend what Carter's done. But I'll always defend myself and my ability to control my fate, now and until the day I die. "I *finally* have a choice," I tell him with a hardened voice, seeing my friend for the first time as my enemy.

"Is that what you call it?" he questions me.

"I can hide away. I can run. Or, I can know I have enemies and be prepared for what they'll do to me," I tell him staring into his eyes and not backing down. My shoulders shake from the sheer adrenaline and I can barely contain myself. "I don't want you to be an enemy."

"Aria," he breathes my name with agony. "I will never be your enemy."

"Then understand that I will not leave him." I question telling him the whole truth as he stares into my gaze. I don't want to know what he thinks of it, but I need him to know. "I love him, Nikolai."

"You're sick," he tells me with nothing but sadness in his broken gaze. "I won't let you go like this." His voice begs me to understand, but I know there's no reasoning with him. Just as there's no reasoning with me.

"Maybe I am sick," I play along with him and somewhere deep in my soul, I even agree. "But wasn't I sick all along? Hiding away in my room and afraid of everything." The defensiveness in my voice is nothing compared to the anger I feel at remembering how pathetic my life used to be. Life might be too kind a word to describe what I had before Carter took me.

"That's why I tried to save you," Nik tells me and reaches for my hand, but I pull away. His fingers brushing against mine feel like a fire that burns deep into the bone.

The cords in his throat tighten as he watches the space between us grow and he confesses, "I wanted you to be free. You deserve to live a better life than this."

His words ring in my ears and echo over and over. It fills the hollowness in the crevices of my chest. *He tried to save me?*

"You what?" I breathe the question.

Everything slows to a crawl as he answers, a look of shame showing on his face. "This," he motions with his hands, "this is all my fault." He struggles to look me in the eye when he tells me, "I knew you'd think it was Mika. I wanted you out, so you could run, but Cross lied to me."

My heartbeat ticks in slow motion. So slowly, the world tilts on its axis and I feel lightheaded. I have to grip the table to stay upright.

"He said he would get you out. He promised me he'd save you. He fucking lied to me, and I fell for it!" He contains his resentment when I don't respond, and leans forward begging me to understand, "All I ever wanted was for you to be free from this. I won't let this ruin you. You deserve so much better than this."

I can't speak. I can't move. I can't even breathe as I hold onto the table to keep me upright.

"Aria?" Eli calls out my name, but I don't look at him. I don't look at Nikolai when he begs me to forgive him. All I can do is stare at a scratch on the steel card table and try to hold on to my sanity.

"You were my friend," I whisper as tears prick my eyes. This all happened because of him. Because of the one person I had in life. The one person I thought I could fully trust.

"I love you, Aria, and you need to run." The word run makes my lips twitch. *Run*. That's how little he thinks of me. To him, I'm merely a scared girl who needs saving. A girl who should run, not one worthy of staying and fighting.

Letting my gaze find his, I peer into his soft blue eyes and whisper, "You don't know who I am anymore."

"You're innocent in this. You're too innocent for this life."

"Nothing about me is innocent, Nikolai. It's only what you all *think* of me."

"You know that it's not--" Nik tries to backpedal but I cut him off. I'm tired of being the scared little girl. I refuse to be seen as such.

"I never knew I had a choice until it was taken from me. I won't let anyone take it back."

"I can make this right, Aria," Nik reaches for my hand again, leaving his palm up on the table. And I take it willingly because I still love him, even if he's made all the wrong choices and doesn't see it. I still love him. He may not know how I've changed, but the boy inside of him is the same. My friend is staring back at me. I know that much.

I rub soothing strokes on the back of his hand as I look him in the eyes, letting my anger go and knowing he will never agree with me. My voice is hoarse as I whisper, "I'm fine, Nikolai."

"You're not. I can see you clearly, Aria. I always have." His voice begs me to listen, and I am, I just don't agree.

"I wish I was a better man, so I could save you. I tried," he tells me even though he looks past me with disappointment and regret equal in his expression. "I tried."

My heart pains for his. He'll never understand, and I don't know what this means for us, but I know this meeting was useless for this war.

"Try to move the men on Carlisle. I can save myself." My response gets his attention, and he shoots me a halfhearted smile, but one from a friend to a friend. One that warms the chill that runs through me.

"You're not doing a very good job of that, Ria." He uses the same nickname my mother had for me and it breaks the wall of strength I've been holding on to.

"It's been so long since someone's called me that," I tell him with a smile that matches his.

"I'll always love you," he tells me and he grips my hand harder. He whispers, "Always, Ria," before kissing my wrist. A move that makes Eli shift his stance once again.

His smile dies before mine does. "I will never

forgive myself if something happens to you," he says, and his voice is choked. "I can't do anything now, but I promise I'll make this right, even if you hate me for it."

"I wish you would just listen to me," I tell him as the door opens behind me. The rusty hinges make it known without turning my head to see.

"I'll make it right," Nikolai says hurriedly as two men walk around the table on either side of me and take him away. I have to grip the edge of my seat to keep from reaching for him. My heart splinters, not knowing when I'll see him again and feeling as if I've failed miserably.

"Don't be stupid, Nikolai," I call after him.

He peeks over his shoulder at me with a smile that I recognize and one that brings tears to prick the back of my eyes. "I'll try not to, Ria."

"You'll let him go?" I ask Eli quickly and with a desperation that's obvious.

He doesn't hesitate to answer, "So long as he doesn't do anything stupid."

I can only nod a response, not trusting myself to speak, knowing full well Nikolai would do foolish things to save me.

The door closes, and Eli tells me we're waiting for a moment, but I hardly hear him as I think about everything that was revealed in the last thirty minutes.

I never thought much of who I wanted to be as I got older. I only knew what I was running from.

I didn't want to marry someone my father approved of, like Mika. I never wanted that, and I thought if I stayed quiet and listened, my father wouldn't marry me off as some of the whispers I'd heard hinted at that possibility.

I didn't want to be the reason the man I fell in love with died. That's the exact reason Nikolai and I ended what we had. When my father started watching me closely, when he asked me if anyone had touched me because he'd kill them if they had, I denied it.

And when he cornered Nikolai and asked him, Nikolai told my father what he wanted to hear, that we were nothing but friends, but he would honor my father's request to leave me alone.

I knew I didn't want to be alone; I didn't want to run away. And so, I sat there in my room, quietly hiding from everything I knew I didn't want, but I never thought of what I wanted. I never chased what I knew deep down could be mine.

Nothing will stop me from chasing it now.

CHAPTER 13

Carter

"Whiskey?" Daniel asks me as I watch Aria's throat tighten as she stares at the table. She did well, but still, watching it was fucking agony.

"Give her a minute," I speak into the microphone to Eli as I nod at Daniel. The amber liquid swirls in the bottle and reflects the pale moonlight filtering into my office.

Sitting back in my chair, I refuse to acknowledge how on edge my body feels. I'm on the edge of breaking down once again. My throat is dry and tight, my fingers and toes numb.

"She loves him," I admit the truth that splinters my chest in a whisper as I stare at the screen. It was clear to see in the way she spoke to him and held him and comforted him. But more than that, it's obvious he loves her as well.

That's something I can't allow.

"I don't want to hear you talk about the woman you love, not in that context. Not about her loving someone else." Daniel's response leaves no room for negotiation and I turn to him as he hands the tumbler to me.

Bringing the glass to my lips, I know what he's referring to and maybe it makes me coldhearted, but the pain that lies in between his words brings me comfort. The whiskey burns my chest as I tilt back the glass and take it all at once.

"Another?" I ask him, holding out the glass for him to refill even though his is still very much full. Three fingers' worth of whiskey is still evident in his glass.

He fills mine higher than before; the bottle that was full only two days ago is nearly empty now. As I take a large swig, I can hear his blunt nails tapping rhythmically against the glass. He leans against the window behind me rather than taking his seat.

"You have all of his files, so you could blackmail him into leaving." Daniel offers me a way to take care of the pesky problem. It's a solution that would work for most people, but not for Nikolai.

"He's irrational," I answer him, knowing all too well Nikolai won't stand down.

"You mean stupid?" he jokes, and I give him a rough chuckle in response, but the smirk that tries to tug at my lips ultimately fails to show itself.

"Do you think she'll hate me now that she knows I set her up all along?" I ask him. The nerves roil in my gut, and I shut them up with another swig. That's what I'm truly worried about. Everything else is meaningless. But that piece of information could hurt us. Romano set it all up, technically, creating the meeting between the two of us. But I'm guilty and won't refute what he told Aria.

"I'm sure she already blamed you." Although there's a hint of humor in his answer, the truth of it causes my blood to turn to ice.

I scoff as I watch as my songbird stand, pushing in the chair and staring long and hard at the empty one across from her before preparing to leave. She doesn't stop staring at where Nikolai was sitting and every second her gaze stays there, the crack in my heart feels like dry lightning splitting the sky into two.

"She loves you," Daniel says from behind me, but it doesn't offer me any comfort.

"Will she when this is over?" The question alone causes the pain to run up my spine and I put the glass to my lips, only to find it empty. With a sigh, I place it on the desk.

The truth is, I don't think she will.

"I'm more concerned with her giving orders and trying to interfere, aren't you?" Daniel questions. Glancing over my shoulder, I watch my brother sip the whiskey although his eyes stay on mine.

"She can do as she wishes," I tell him the same thing I've told Eli. "I want to see what she'll do."

"She's different than I thought."

I feel restless as I watch his gaze flick to the screen, no longer focused on the back room and instead, watching Eli accompany Aria back to the safe house. Men are in multiple homes spread throughout the two blocks and each of them has eyes on her as they move from street to street.

"How's that?" I question him.

Bringing his gaze back to mine, he sets his glass on the windowsill and tells me, "She's... more..." he chooses his words carefully, "*involved* than I thought she'd be." The nervousness that prickles down my fingers intensifies when he adds, "I'm not sure what to make of it."

Cracking my knuckles, I don't look him in the eyes when I respond, "It means she'll be even more disappointed when all of it is over."

My brother considers me for a moment before nodding once and picking up his glass to finish off the drink.

He runs his fingers along the rim of the empty glass, watching as he does so and tells me, "I'm taking Addison out for the night." His lips pull down into a frown and his eyes reflect a well of sadness. "She hasn't been to The Hard Stone." He finally looks up to me and I nod, letting him know I heard him. The Hard Stone is the restaurant next to the Red Room. It's heavily guarded already, as is the club.

"I hope it goes well," I offer him, and it's genuine. I hate what's happened to them. I don't want to see my brother revert back to the man he is without her. There are only two versions of him. And I greatly prefer the one who is loved by Addison and loves her in return.

Running my thumb over the pad of my pointer, I think about Aria being all alone tonight and how she'll be thinking of Nikolai.

"Keep her out late," I tell Daniel, waiting for his eyes to reach mine. "Don't come back to the safe house for a few hours."

He lips are slow to pull into a smile, but they do.

"Do you have plans with your girl as well?" he asks me with a sense of humor that lights his eyes.

"I do now."

CHAPTER 14

Aria

IT'S QUIET. Too quiet.

The kind of quiet that makes you feel unsettled deep inside. Staring down at the empty glass of wine, I bite down on my bottom lip knowing full well that it doesn't matter if it's quiet or if I was in a room full of people chattering because I was going to feel like this tonight regardless.

This sick, numbing feeling spreads over every inch of me the second I'm consciously aware and not drifting down a memory I wish I could hide in.

Letting out a deep sigh, I push the glass away from me and wrap the woven blanket tighter around my shoulders as I get off the barstool at the kitchen island.

I finally ate today, but the food's tasteless and I can barely stomach a thing. Not when I feel like this.

Addison left half an hour ago, and I asked Eli to tell the guys to leave me alone tonight. Part of me regrets it. I'd like to pretend I could go downstairs and join them for a drink. Lord knows I need more than just one glass of Cabernet. I need a distraction and something that doesn't feel like my world is falling apart and collapsing on top of me, but that's all I have to accompany me tonight.

My bare feet pad softly on the hardwood floor as I make my way down the hall to the bedroom. All I keep thinking about is the phone on the nightstand. It only allows me to call Carter, or for Carter to call me. There's not even a number in the settings for me to give someone else.

I hate that he limits me like this, but I understand the need for him to control it right now. Because if I could, I'd call my father. I'd tell him I'm sorry I left and was stupidly taken. I'd tell him I'm okay. I'd beg him to stop all this.

And I'd be judged, found lacking, and a failure. I already know it, but I would still try.

Just the thought of it makes me pause outside the bedroom door, my hand on the carved glass knob as a shuddering breath leaves me. I hate this feeling of hopelessness that numbs my skin. I hate this feeling of being confined and pushed to the side.

I hate everything.

When the door creaks open, my feet sink into the

plush carpet and I try to flick the light on, but it doesn't work.

My stomach drops even lower and I try it again, hearing the click but not seeing a change. It doesn't stop me from furiously flicking the switch back and forth rapidly.

"I didn't want any light tonight." Carter's voice paralyzes my body. It's a slow drip, like the venom from a snake bite. That's how my body reacts to his deep, rough tone.

It takes a moment for my eyes to adjust, but when they do, I see his broad shoulders from the corner of the room, sitting on a chair that wasn't there this morning.

"Carter," I say his name and then glance at the mess of sheets on the bed, and he follows my gaze to where I was hours ago, pleasuring myself as he ordered me to. "I didn't expect you to be here," I tell him softly and make my way toward him.

It amazes me how drawn I am to him. As if nothing matters but going to him.

Maybe Nikolai was right. Maybe I am sick. Because all that nervousness and anxiety doesn't exist anymore.

"I missed you," he tells me, and it sounds so unlike the man I knew while I was in the cell, and the man who rules with an iron fist but it's my Carter, the man who gives me everything behind closed doors. Flutters in the pit of my stomach travel up higher and lower at the same time, warming every inch of me.

"I need you," I whisper as I reach him, not hesitating

to climb into his lap and wrap my legs around his waist. His large hands splay along my lower back and ass. He squeezes just as my lips brush against his and instead of kissing him like I intended, my neck arches back and I moan from the pain.

From the pain.

It's all he gives me at this moment, but sitting like this, being with him and feeling his heat is exactly what I need right now. The pain alone sends ripples of pleasure through my body.

He lowers his lips to the dip in my throat, letting his stubble drag along my skin as he plants open-mouth kisses right there and then trails up my neck.

He nips my earlobe before whispering in a way that creates a shiver down my spine, "I want you on the bed."

I take a kiss from him first. Stealing it quickly, I love that I catch him off guard and he nearly misses the chance to kiss me back.

He takes it though and then sits back as I leave his lap and lie on the bed.

"Strip," he commands, and I obey. I do it slowly, letting my fingers linger over my sensitized skin and reveling in the power I have. He wants me. He loves wanting me. And it's a heady feeling to have such a powerful man give in to the need of wanting you.

The clothes fall carelessly to the floor and the cool air kisses my skin as I writhe on the bed and run the tips of my fingers over my hardened nipples.

Carter stands slowly, and I barely turn my head to

watch him stalk around the bed, stripping slowly for me as well. With the only light coming from the windows behind me, the shadows dance around him and it's intoxicating.

I can hear the clink of handcuffs before I see the metal shine in the pale moonlight, and it only makes me hotter for him. Before he commands me to, I raise my arms above my head and to the headboard made of thin planks. He only uses a single pair of cuffs, looping them through the planks and cuffing each of my wrists.

His fingers burn along my wrists and he lets them travel down my arm, tickling me, my breasts, my waist and then he dips a hand between my legs and I spread myself wide for him.

The groan deep in his throat is my reward, as is the spread of pleasure that runs through my body when he trails his thick fingers from my hot entrance up to my clit.

Writhing on the bed sends a mix of pain from the belt marks rubbing against the sheets and the pleasure from his touch.

He leaves me like that, breathing heavily on edge for him for a moment to grab something from the floor.

A tie, his tie. The silk runs along my cheek and then he tells me to close my eyes as he wraps it around me like a blindfold. My heart races at not being able to see and a new kind of excitement courses through my body.

Without being able to see, I can hear it clearly when he takes out another cuff as his fingers travel down my leg, to my ankle where he cuffs me. He does the same to the other side and I'm blindfolded and restrained for him.

My breathing comes in chaotically when I hear him walk around the bed again and the cold metal heats while the chill in the air makes me beg him to be touched. "Carter," I whimper his name.

"Tell me the truth, songbird." Carter's voice is deep. but laced with something I haven't heard from him in the bedroom for so long. A hard edge I don't like to hear.

Although my heart batters in my chest with the mix of fear slipping into my veins, I whisper, "Anything."

"You hate me, don't you?" he asks me and with his question comes a click and buzzing. My back bows as he touches the cold metal of the vibrator to my clit. The pleasure is immediate and spikes through me.

"I love you," I moan recklessly into the air as I pull at my cuffs, unable to move away from the intense pleasure.

He pushes it harder against me and I let out a strangled cry of ecstasy. I can feel myself clench around nothing as the intense waves of pleasure approach like the tide, creeping up and crashing harder and harder.

I'm so close. So, fucking close.

And then he pulls it away.

A gasp is torn from me and I try to look around. I want to hear where he is and what he's doing over the sound of my own ragged breath. But as I do, my impending orgasm slowly dims, leaving me slick with my own arousal and desperate for him to get me off.

Swallowing down the disappointment and trying not to pull on the cuffs that dig into my wrists and ankles, I wait for him.

"You hated me when you came to the cell."

I breathe in deeply, not wanting to remember how we started. My voice is raspy when I tell him, "I knew I wanted you."

His thick fingers push inside of me and I can feel his knuckles brush against my front wall. My breasts swing, and my shoulder blades dig into the mattress as he finger-fucks me. "Fuck," I moan, feeling the warmth spread through my body like wildfire as the bundle of nerves in my core heat and prepare to ignite.

"Carter," I breathe his name as my neck arches and I feel the pleasure build higher and higher. "Carter," I moan his name just before I cum.

And he pulls away before I can finish. My breathing's chaotic and I try to rip the blindfold away, but my hands are cuffed.

"Carter!" I yell at him and all I get in return is a rough chuckle. He kisses my jaw even as I pull away from him.

"I don't like this," I warn him in a voice that wavers. I can feel a sense of dread flow into my blood.

"All you have to do is answer me." His voice is easy as if this isn't a trap. "Did you hate me?" he asks again, and my voice tightens.

The buzzing gets louder and this time the vibrator

hits me at full force. My head pushes back and the pleasure races through my blood. I'm so close. I'm already on the edge with only a few seconds of its touch.

And then it's taken away. Gritting my teeth, I struggle to move, feeling tears prick my eyes. "Carter!" I scream at him with unadulterated anger, but all I get is the vibrator back on my swollen nub.

Again, he takes it away just before the pleasure can consume me, leaving me with dimming fire and I can't fucking take it.

"Yes, I hated you! You hurt me, and I hated you for taking me!"

The pain that sweeps through me is like nothing I've felt before. Admitting what happened and knowing what I felt back then... I hate it. I hate that he's bringing it up. "Is that what you wanted?" I ask him, furious that he's doing this. "I hate this!" I yell at him but as the last word leaves my lips, the vibrator hits my clit and he leaves it there, my body flying higher and higher and then I fall from the sky, sending a tingling sensation to wreck my body all at once.

It lasts and lasts as I lie paralyzed and still at Carter's mercy.

"You loved me afterward though?" he asks me, his lips so close to mine and I push myself up as high as I can and steal his lips with mine. He kisses me back ravenously. I can feel his body close to mine and I wish I could wrap my legs around him and hold on to him, but I'm bound, and he pulls away from me.

I'm still reeling from my orgasm and the kiss I was

too starved for to remember what he asked me, so he asks me again.

Breathlessly, I answer him, "Yes, I love you. I love you, Carter."

As his name leaves my lips, he pushes the vibrator back to my sensitized bud and it's nearly too much. I scream his name and he captures my lips with his as I detonate beneath him. The pleasure consumes me as the night sky is consumed with stars. Again and again.

I want to kiss him, but more than anything I want him to know how much I mean it when I say it. I love him, and he's all I want.

"Do you love Nikolai?" he asks me, and the question destroys the moment. I struggle to answer, but I do know the truth and I won't lie to him.

"Yes. But not like you," I answer him, feeling the high fall and my pulse slow. A second passes and another without him making a sound or touching me and fear races through my blood. "Carter?" I call out his name and he asks me another question.

"If I wasn't here, would you be with him?"

The silence stretches as I remember wanting Nikolai but being too afraid to tell my father. That girl, the one who doesn't go after what she wants and simply prays not to be seen, that girl is long dead.

"I don't know," I answer him in a breath and again he denies me, pushing the vibrator to my clit and finger-fucking me until I'm so close to my release I can't breathe.

Gasping for air, I search for some kind of relief,

brushing my ass against the silky sheets, but Carter tsks me, holding my hips down.

"Just tell me the truth, songbird. I'll take care of you," he whispers in a voice I don't trust. One that's sinful.

"I don't know Carter. Please," I try to beg him, but he doesn't listen. He presses the vibrator against my clit and pulls away nearly instantaneously. My body bucks and the metal bites into my skin. "Fuck!" I cry out. I'm so close. I'm so fucking close again.

Off and on, off and on, he teases me.

The tides of my pleasure rush to the surface, igniting every nerve ending, but as soon as they're ready to go off, he pulls away and waits for the embers to die before bringing the fire back.

"If I wasn't here, would you be with him?" he asks me softly, calmly, his lips close to the shell of my ear. His breath traveling along my skin is enough to nearly get me off. I don't answer, I only bite down on my lower lip and shake my head, but I can't answer him.

And he does it again. Finger-fucking me ruthlessly, but the second my orgasm approaches, he pulls away. The smell of sex and the feel of my slickness on my inner thighs tease me into thinking there's more. But he leaves me panting and again my orgasm dies before I can get off.

It's the last bit I can take.

"Yes! I would try to be with Nikolai if you were gone." I can hardly believe I've spoken the sin out loud, much less to Carter. I know it hurts him and I hate it. I fucking hate it, but it's the truth. "I would try to be with him," I suck in a deep breath, brushing the tears off my face away with my forearms and wishing I could do the same with my shame, "but I don't know that I could ever have what we have. I wouldn't be the person I am without you." Tears leak down my face as the confession is forced out of me. "I love you, Carter. I don't want him when I have you."

He ruthlessly strokes against my front wall and I cum instantly. He pulls the orgasm from me, drawing it out and my body arches and goes rigid as the silent scream of ecstasy is ripped from me.

He doesn't stop until I'm limp and struggling to breathe.

"Carter, stop please," I beg him in a strangled voice that doesn't sound at all like me. "I hate this. I chose you! I fucking chose you!"

"Shh," he shushes me as I struggle to breathe. The touch of his splayed hand on my belly makes me jump, but he caresses my skin with soothing strokes until my entire body has calmed. With soft kisses on my neck, I beg him to stop again and let me love him. It's all I want to do right now, love him and feel the love he has for me.

"One more question," he tells me, and I stay as still as I can, waiting for it and dreading it. I can't stop crying, knowing what I've already confessed to him and worried that he won't love me because of it.

"Will you still when your family is gone? Will you still love me then?"

I already know the answer, but I don't want to say it.

The buzz from the vibrator makes me cry harder. He runs it along my pubic bone and my hips buck, trying to move away. I can't take any more.

"Tell me the truth," he whispers in a voice coated in hopelessness. He already knows the answer; I've already told him. He doesn't need to torture it out of me.

"No," I cry out. Hating him for what he's doing. I don't want to think about any of this, let alone admit what it would do to us.

"I love you, but if you do it… if you kill them, I will hate you forever," I gasp out as tears stream down my face. Agony tears through me both in the physical sense and emotional. He wrecked me. Carter destroyed whatever guard I had that protected me from this truth.

"I love you, Carter." I hear the cuffs click and then the metal leaves my skin. It's biting into my wrists and the second he unlocks them; I cradle my wrists to my chest.

I'm still crying into the blindfold when I hear the bedroom door open and shut. The hollowness in my chest collapses on itself and I refuse to believe he left me.

But when I finally take the blindfold off and beg him to hold me, he's not there.

Carter left me.

He doesn't love me. Carter Cross doesn't love me.

CHAPTER 15

Carter

I CAN STILL FEEL her cunt spasming on my cock the first time I took her. I still dream of it.

I can still taste the sweet wine on her lips.

I can still hear her screams of pleasure and her whispers that she loves me.

I know for as long as I live, I'll remember it all. I'll remember what I had with her.

Tonight, I wage war against her family; I'll kill as many of them as I possibly can.

I'll destroy what we have together and risk her hating me forever. She was telling the truth and I can't stand it. Tonight, I will lose the woman I love.

My gaze drops to the phone on the bathroom counter just as Jase knocks on my bedroom door.

"In here," I call out to him and turn on the faucet to wet my razor. The shaving cream is already slathered on my skin. Since leaving her last night, I've fallen back into my old habits and I'm distracting myself by focusing on the war and everything else involved in this business.

He talks as I shave, ridding myself of the stubble and preparing to look the part of a man in control of an empire. "I have a proposition," he starts, and my eyes move to his in the reflection of the mirror before moving back to my jaw.

Each stroke of the blade is precise and smooth, skimming along my skin.

He takes a step forward, filling in the doorway. "I think our problem is that we've been content."

"Our problem?"

"The reason men think they can steal from us, the reason Romano is creating competition and involved us in this war." I consider him for a moment before going back to shaving, tapping the razor against the sink before bringing the blade down my skin again. I couldn't give two shits about any of it anymore. I'll kill those who defy me or stand in my way. And I'll be fucking content with that regardless of whether or not Jase is.

He tells me with a raised brow, "We aren't expanding."

"We have other ventures. The club. The restaurant." I don't know why I bother reminding him. I can see the look in his eyes. He won't stop until he gets what he wants.

"That money doesn't compare. You know, I know, and everyone else knows it." He speaks hurriedly like he can't wait to make his point, but I drag it out. Just to torture him.

"We're moving into Crescent Hills," I tell him.

"Because you want to take on that place, not because there's money there." His voice is flat, his expression expectant.

I can't argue that truth. "It'll be worth it to be closer to the docks," I tell him, and he shakes his head in disagreement. My patience ebbs as I tap my razor again on the sink and hold it under the running water.

"I think we need to go north. A true expansion," he tells me and waits with bated breath.

"Talvery territory?" I question him, my eyes on his in the mirror and he nods his head. "I already gave it to Romano."

"It hasn't been taken yet, and Romano can go fuck himself." Jase's voice is harsh and his persistence shines through. Jase keeps his gaze on me even though he's breathing harder with excitement. "We were going to give Fallbrook to Romano and he already has the entire upper east. Talvery turf should be ours."

His eyes dart over to mine, waiting for a reaction but I give him none. I didn't sleep for shit and I don't give a fuck about expanding.

"Are you that bored?" I ask him dully. I remember what it was like to take control, what was required to have my name permanently carved into this territory.

The sickness of it all and the risk. It's not worth the money it makes.

"Bored?" Jase breathes out forcefully. "It's a lost opportunity." I don't respond. Instead, I finish shaving, careful not to react when Jase adds, "And what about Aria?"

I rip the hand towel from where it hangs at my right and dampen it under the faucet. It's hard to contain what I feel for her. The loss is too real. It's too close.

"What about her?" As I clean off my face, ignoring the screaming pain in my chest, he tells me, "I heard about how she's handling things." I grip the towel tighter, praying my brother doesn't say something that drives me to break his fucking jaw. Last night... I can't even think about how the truth stabbed me in the heart like nothing else has before.

He tells me, "I think she'd want this."

My brow furrows and I focus on breathing and controlling my expressions. "Want what?" Speaking hurts. Even breathing hurts. Everything fucking hurts.

"I think she'd want to still have the territory... maybe for her?" he offers, tilting his head and raising his brow. "Can you imagine how she'd react if we killed her family and gave her land to Romano?"

Using the dry section of the towel, I run it over my jaw, knowing exactly how she's going to react and hating it. I swallow thickly, knowing I can keep her here. Physically, I have the means to keep her here, but that will only add to her hate. And I want her to love me. I need her to love me.

"What if, instead, we do as little damage as possible?" He moves out of the doorway as I toss the towel into the sink and make my way past him to my dresser for my cufflinks. I'm running through the motions, focused on every mundane detail that's led me to this point in life.

"Any damage we do will break her, Jase," I tell him halfheartedly.

"I'm telling you, this is a good idea, Carter."

He stands a few feet from me, leaning against the wall with his arms crossed. "We already told Romano, but I say we hit them back to back. Talvery, then Romano and we take it all."

"With what men?" I ask him, feeling the tingling rage creep up my spine. "Do you remember the cost of it all? How many men have to die for you to be satisfied?" My voice is raised, and my pulse quickens. I swallow back the anger when he doesn't respond.

He flinches at the severity of my tone.

I add, "This isn't a game and every move has consequences."

"It's all a game, brother." He looks me in the eyes as he says, "A well-played and thought-out game."

He stares at me and I him as he tells me, "If Aria was able to convince those men to do what she suggested yesterday, we would have the upper hand. Talvery and Romano would lose men, and we'd be waiting to take out the rest," he talks with an evenness that sounds so reassuring.

"Only Aria doesn't know that," I tell him while

taking a step forward and reaching for my jacket, which is draped across the dresser. "She doesn't know how many will die. And she will never be okay with wiping out her family."

The hint of a smile that was on his lips falters. "She has more to learn," is all he can say.

"Tonight, her family legacy starts to fall, and she will never forgive me, let alone rule alongside me." Jase's smile completely vanishes, and he glances at his feet before looking me back in the eyes, ready to say something else, but I don't let him. "Do you think she'll want to rule when her territory is nothing, but a grave-yard of old memories and people forgotten?"

It fucking kills me knowing how she'll react. "She's going to fucking hate me," I bite out the words, grinding my back teeth against one another.

My breathing is ragged as he nods his head and runs his thumb over his bottom lip. "So, you're saying it's too late?" he asks.

That's exactly how it all feels. It's too late to keep her.

I let his question sit with me as I shrug on the jacket and button it. "I still think she would want this. Even if the war leaves a path of death to her throne, not everyone will die. She'll have some."

"Like Nikolai?" I reply with spite barely above a murmur, and it only makes Jase smirk at me.

"I have a feeling that fellow isn't going to make it," he jokes but it doesn't do anything to soothe the nerves that won't allow me to relax.

"In thirty minutes, they'll open fire," I tell him as I observe the little hand on my watch marching along steadily. "The next time you have an idea about damage control, maybe come to me sooner?" I suggest, and he huffs a laugh while shaking his head.

"The war has only started," he says, not giving up. "Just tell me you'll consider it."

Screwing over Romano is inevitable; doing it at the right time is crucial.

But the worst mistake Jase is assuming is that Talvery can already be counted as dead. I've made that mistake before, and I won't make it again.

"I consider everything, Jase."

CHAPTER 16

Aria

THREE CANVASES ARE SPREAD out across an old bedsheet on the floor of the living room. Three canvases with three profiles on each of them. Two men I love, and my mother, who's long gone make up the three. All the while, my mind focuses on the news that plays on the television in the background.

The list of names goes on and on. I can't look at the faces. I can't look at the scenes as they show them on the screen.

Addison is cuddled up on the sofa, staring blankly at the TV. The names don't mean anything to her, but to me, each name means far too much.

I'm barely holding myself together, knowing I

should be at their funerals. Knowing I failed to save them. There's a mix of contempt and dread for Nikolai. I wonder if he even tried to move them. He knew, and what did he do? I remember what he said though, it was an army he didn't control.

It's only a matter of time before his name is spoken, added to the mounting death toll of the senseless murders between rival gangs, or so the reporter tells us on the flat-screen TV. Even the thought, forces me to choke on a dry sob, but I hold it down.

"Does this happen a lot?" Addison asks me, and I can feel her eyes on my back, but I don't trust myself to look at her, so instead, I place the flat brush in the cup and watch the red pigment bleed into the water.

"No, not like this," I answer her with my back to her. I am so used to death that it shouldn't break me like this. But it's the first time I tried to stop it.

And I failed.

"Do you need anything else?" Eli's voice comes from the doorway to the stairwell and I peek up at him, but I don't respond. He got me the paints from the corner store a few blocks down. The other things were in the package from Carter. I need a lot of things, I think. But as my lips pull down into a frown and my throat goes tight, I don't look back at him. Instead, I just shake my head no.

I hate him for standing by and doing nothing while men are dying. I hate myself for hating him, which is even worse.

"I want to go get them myself," I tell him as the

thought hits me. I need to get out of here and go for a walk. I need to clear my head. I need something. I squeeze the cheap bristles over the cup before rinsing it again. "It would be nice to get some fresh air." I'm surprised by how even my voice is and how in control I seem. It's only because of Addison. If she weren't here, I have no idea how I would react to tonight.

The metal ferrule that holds the bristles clinks softly on the side of the glass as I tap it and then set it down gently on the paper towel.

I finally look up again and Eli's watching me closely. Addison's looking between the two of us and the air is tense among all three of us. She doesn't ask questions though and tonight, I can feel anger growing inside of me from her not wanting to know any more than whether or not this is normal.

"I want to go for a walk to the corner store, so I can buy a few things... please," I say the last word through clenched teeth.

"Give me an hour," Eli responds and then adds, "please." He mocks me, but in a way I know is meant to ease the tension. It doesn't though.

Giving him a tight smile, I nod once and watch him leave, although I still can't find an even breath. Everything is tense, and nothing is right. I feel like I'm breaking down. I'm losing it every second I sit here, guarded and watching the list of deaths grow.

"Are you okay?" Addie asks me as the sound of Eli's footsteps diminishes.

"No," I answer her honestly.

I wanted to help my family, and Nikolai ignored me.

I told Carter I loved him, I chose to stay with him, and he left me.

I'm a fool. I'm a fucking fool.

I'm helpless, hopeless and I feel like I'm at my limit.

The sofa groans as Addie slips off of it and makes her way toward me. She's quiet as she sits cross-legged next to me and leans in to give me a hug.

"I wish I knew what to say or do," she consoles me in a quiet voice and I instantly regret the thoughts I had moments ago. I'm so eager to lash out, I could see her being the misguided target of my frustrations, but I would never forgive myself.

Grabbing on to her forearm and giving her a semblance of a hug back, I tell her, "I wish I knew too."

Time passes slowly until she grabs the remote and turns off the TV. The click of the picture going black is louder than I've ever heard it before. I want it to stay on, so I'll know what happened, but I'm grateful she turned it off because I can't take any more.

"Do you want to talk?" she asks me, and I shake my head. I'm ashamed of how much of myself I give to Carter, only to have him hold back in return. I don't think I could tell her without her hating him even more. And after the night she had with Daniel, I couldn't do that to her.

"You could distract me and tell me what happened last night again," I offer, feeling a swell of jealousy and pain grow in my chest. Last night, I felt used. For the first time, I felt used and foolish for loving him.

"It was just a good night," Addie says, moving her hands to her lap. I know she doesn't want to rub it in, so I just nod and let it go. I stare at the doorway as if Eli will magically appear and let me go outside. The thought makes me roll my eyes. I'm stupid to think I had any sense of control.

Before I can spiral down the path to self-pity that kept me up all last night, Addison asks me, "Do you want to read my tarot cards?"

I watch her chew on the inside of her cheek, waiting for an answer. I'm so grateful for her that I would do anything she asked right now. For the distraction, for the genuine friendship, and so I nod.

"Let's do it," I answer her.

With a deep breath, I scoot backward and turn to her, sitting opposite her and cross-legged too as she reaches behind her on the coffee table for the deck of cards Carter got me however long ago.

"Okay, what do I do?" Addison asks, placing the deck of cards in front of her and staring at them like they'll magically shuffle themselves.

"Knock on them first," I tell her in a deadpan tone, knowing full well she's going to look up at me like I'm crazy.

"I'm serious," I say again and nod to the cards, folding my own hands in my lap. "You have to knock on them to get rid of any previous readings and put your own energy into the cards."

She does what I tell her, lifting the deck and knocking weakly on the back card although she's grinning the entire time. Already I feel a thread better. Only a thread, but it's one more than I had before.

"Now shuffle the deck and think about something you'd like insight to. Or don't." I shrug and stretch from where I'm sitting, feeling the ache from leaning over the canvases for the past few hours. Just glancing at them reminds me about everything and I'm quick to turn back to Addison.

"Is that enough?" she asks me, holding out the cards and I offer her a soft smile and then gesture to the deck. "Split them into three piles, however, you want, and then stack them on top of each other into one pile again."

"Is this how it's always done?" she asks me while doing as I say.

"No," I tell her, feeling a deep ache in my chest. "I learned to read cards from my mother. But she didn't do it like this."

"Oh, how did she do it?" she asks me, and I have to grab the cards and look at them rather than in her eyes when I tell her, "I don't remember. I just had to learn on my own when I decided I wanted to use her deck."

It's quiet for a moment, but she continues the conversation, steering it to a more positive side. "Are these hers?" she asks me as I lay out the cards one by one.

"No, these are ones that Carter got me." Somehow

that pulls even more emotion from me as I set the final card down. I don't tell her that I was locked in a cell losing my mind when I was given these cards. And that Jase is the one who actually gave them to me. That day, or night, comes back to me and I nearly get sick.

"This is the horseshoe spread," I tell her as I lay out the cards, refusing to fall backward; I won't go backward. "The significator is in the center, but each place in this spread has a unique meaning and the seven other cards are spread in a horseshoe around it. The significator, this card, is basically you at this moment."

"The four of wands is me?" she asks me although her eyes are on the card I'm currently touching the edges of.

I nod and then add, "There are four suits: the swords, the wands, the pentacles, also known as coins, and the cups. They each represent something different in life and the wands represent creativity. Swords are conflict, pentacles are money, thus also being called coins, and the cups are emotional wellbeing. More or less.

"The four of wands in this deck— "

"I feel like this is a professional reading," Addison exclaims, barely holding in her excitement and I have to give her a small laugh.

"I've read a lot about cards. A few years ago, I thought it would bring me closer to my mother." I wish I hadn't said that last bit, but Addison doesn't focus on the negative. Instead, she says, "Well, this is freaking awesome." She reaches behind her for the glass of wine and then sits up at attention. "Please, continue." She gestures comically and takes a sip of her wine.

I have to let out a snicker that's almost a snort and remember where I left off. "Right," I say out loud, "The four of wands. In this deck, the four of wands is a literal marriage." As I say the last word, I breathe in deep, realizing how emotional Addison's been and watch her reaction, but she only sips her wine and listens. It takes a lot of pressure off of me, so I continue.

Some people take the cards literally, but I have a feeling Addison won't. She just wants a distraction, just as I do.

"The significator is a snapshot of who you are right now and the four of wands is a resting point. There's been a sense of accomplishment, and there's a sense of celebration over it, thus a marriage as the picture on the card. It's a deeply happy card about solidifying some sense of community. Which may not seem at all like where you are in this moment," I pause, feeling a wave of insecurity, but I continue, giving her the reading I think this card points to, "but it can also mean friendship, solidifying a friendship."

"So, it's us?" she asks me, and I try to keep my voice even and devoid of the intense emotion that rises inside of me when I tell her, "Yeah. I think this card is about us."

Addison settles into her position, an elbow on each knee and tells me, "I like that."

With a deep breath, I point to the first card of the seven that makes the horseshoe. "This is your immediate past and this card, the six of pentacles, is a card of generosity and harmony. It's a card depicting someone who was in a good place with the in and outflow of their money, but it doesn't always refer to money. It can also refer to charity and gracefully accepting or giving of money, time or safety." I pause and swallow before adding, "Like how you helped me. That's what this card could mean."

Addison only nods and takes another sip of wine, so I keep going, moving through the motions rather than thanking her again and bringing up that awful night.

"The immediate present, the next card, is the priestess card. She's a figure who has deep intuition."

"What about the suits? What suit is she?" Addison interrupts and it's only then that I really know she gives a fuck about the card reading or at least she's paying attention.

"The suits are in the minor part of the deck; the major part of the deck has figures basically. So, they aren't a part of the suits. There are basically two types of cards, suits, the minor cards, and then figures, the major cards."

"Oh." She nods and then clears her throat before looking at the other cards in the deck to see how many others are major cards and minor, I assume. "Okay, so the immediate present, is the priestess?"

I nod and then smirk as she adds, "I like that too. So far, this is a very likable reading."

My shoulders shake with a huff of laughter as I continue. "The priestess is a person with deep intuition and she's kind of a major arcana echo of the queen of wands. So, not only does she have a deep intuition about herself, but she has it about other people. In other cards, she's pictured holding a mirror that she can point to herself or to others. She's someone who has otherworldly energies and someone who can observe others for who they are. And also see what they need instinctually."

"Like how I knew Daniel was the man he is?" Addison asks me in a flat tone as she pulls the sleeve of her shirt over her wrist and then wipes under her eyes. With my mouth parted, I'm shocked by her response and I struggle to answer her quickly enough. "Ignore me, I'm sorry." She breathes in deeply and shakes out her wrists. "Sorry, I just had a moment."

"It's okay," I barely speak the words and look back down at the card. "It could mean lots of things," I tell her and then shrug. "Or nothing at all."

"I knew," she tells me with a grief that darkens her eyes. A sad smile graces her lips and she says, "Don't stop, please. For the love of God, let's move past that one."

Clearing my throat, I move on to the next card, but then decide to move back to the priestess. "It could also mean that you know what people need and I don't know your story, but knowing you, I would think you knew he needed you." Addison stares at me with glassy eyes but only nods.

My place isn't between them, so I move back the spread, to the third card in the horseshoe and the immediate future. "The king of wands is your immediate future. The kings in the deck are the last of the suits and they have control over the suits. The pages learn, the knights chase, the queen embodies and the king controls. And so, the king of wands is someone who's able to understand and empathize with creativity and life, but he, himself, is not personally creative or spiritual in a really emphatic sense. Instead, he's someone who works closely with creative or spiritual people, but he's distant from them and that's what makes him good at what he does. It's the distance that allows him to be there for others, but it also prevents him from being a part of it."

Struggling to place this card in the current context, I think back on other meanings for the card.

"The king of wands can also be a person who's charismatic but reserved. Still waters run deep in this person, but he's distant."

"So, someone who's controlling is coming?" Addison asks flatly and then snorts into her wine. "I didn't need cards to tell me that one."

I shake my head, knowing she's referring to Carter or Daniel, but this card wouldn't be either of them. It's someone else. "Someone who's distant and uninvolved," I correct her and feel a chill run along my skin. It pricks every nerve and forces each small hair along my skin to stand on edge.

I can hear her swallow the wine and instead of

asking who or considering the meaning, I simply keep going to the very bottom of the horseshoe and the fourth card. She doesn't object.

"This card, your path, is the eight of swords. And in my deck at home..." I pause and almost regret saying home, but I don't acknowledge it. Thankfully, Addison doesn't press me. "In my mother's deck, the eight of swords depicts Queen Guinevere, she's tied to the stake and she's going to be executed for infidelity. And the interesting thing about the eight of swords is that often you'll see the woman is holding her own bindings around the pole. Different decks have different art though." I take a moment to look at the deck that Carter got me and it's not obvious in this card. "You can't really see it here, but it looks like this woman is trapped to such a horrible fate in the eight of swords, but actually the only thing that's trapping her is herself. She's the one who has to be able to let go and free herself from her restraints." I look at the card again and realize it doesn't look like that on this deck and it's the only deck I've ever seen where the bonds are truly tied. I continue though, refusing to let her think she's tied inextricably to this fate.

"The woman in this card is not going to be rescued, but she's not doomed to this terrible fate either. The only thing trapping her is herself. The good news is that she's able to save herself; she's not actually tied to the stake."

I take a moment, thinking about everything as

Addison finishes off her wine and doesn't say a word. *These cards could be for me.* The idea that they are sends a shiver down my spine. Addison knocked on the cards, I remind myself. Without a word from Addison and not liking where my thoughts are headed, I continue.

"The perceptions of others is the next card, the fifth spot in the horseshoe. The knight of wands is your card in this spot. The knight of wands is all about deep fire and chasing. Do first, think later. They tend to be impulsive."

Addison laughs into her empty glass as she twirls the stem of it between two fingers. "Sounds like that one could be true," she says with a smile on her lips and I can't help but smile too.

"The next card is the challenge to be faced and this is an interesting card to be sitting here." I think out loud, not censoring anything. "The nine of cups is on the cusp of culminating happiness. It's the difference between being engaged and being married. There's anticipation that there's something that's still held back. And then the next card, the ten is complete happiness and marriage, nothing left to come."

Addison nods all the while that I explain the card and I'm not sure how she's perceiving it until she speaks.

"So, there's still more to come? More that would make me happy?"

"Well this is the challenge card, so that's the obstacle

you're facing." My answer tugs her lips down and her gaze moves toward the cards. "So, the challenge here is that you're almost there, but not quite and that's where the tension is." I don't stop. I don't want her to think about it right now, but I don't think she'd tell me even if she had ideas of what the cards could mean.

"The final card is the outcome, and for you, it's the queen of wands. She's someone who is safe, confident and she's able to empathize and nurture but she's also powerful and creative in her own right. She's someone who can wield power, but also stands on her own two feet. She's the fiery enchantress."

"That's my final outcome? I get to be a fiery enchantress?" she jokes but I'm so relieved the reading seems to be ending on a happy note.

With a nod, I tell her, "Yes, Addie. You get to be the fiery enchantress." I can't keep my face straight as I tell her that.

"So, when does that happen?" she asks me, and I have to snort a laugh while smiling.

"The priestess in the present position means this person often holds this role. It's also a major arcana card and that typically means it takes time, but it's in the immediate present position. That means there's something otherworldly about her, so she's always carrying this inside of her. Everything else is minor arcana so that would mean days… maybe weeks. But probably days." My gaze falls back to the king of wands and my blood chills. *Someone is coming.*

Addison smiles and bites down on the edge of her wine glass as she glances at the cards one last time.

Again, the king of wands is all I can see, and I'm focused so intently although I don't want to be. He calls to me. The distanced man who's coming and a chill flows down my spine in a way that feels like a nail raking down my back.

"If you're done," Eli's voice breaks through my thoughts and I've never been more grateful.

"Yes," I'm quick to tell him as Addison collects the cards, quickly putting them back on top of the deck. She seems to be just as absorbed with the card as well. I watch as she stacks all the cards neatly in the deck and puts him down last, right at the end of the deck.

"Do you want me to come with you?" Addison asks me as I push up off the floor, shaking out my hands and nerves, and try to shake off the uneasy feeling creeping along my skin. The tiny hairs at the back of my neck refuse to go unnoticed. They don't leave me alone; even as I walk across the room and put the jean jacket on, the chill stays with me.

"I think I'm going to try to sleep then," she tells me although I think she said it more to herself. She covers her face when she says, "I need that stuff, though."

"The stuff?" I ask her to clarify as I stop a few feet from Eli and think back to the vial of sweet lullabies. The drug he gave me to sleep.

"Daniel gave it to me because I wasn't sleeping, and I don't know what I did with it." She looks at the coffee table as if she left it there, but there's nothing there.

"It gave me nightmares. The lullaby stuff."

"That's a shame," she says with true pity. "I slept so well with it. And today has been…" she doesn't finish, she only shakes her head. I can only imagine how she's feeling. I know she wants to go back to Daniel. I could see it in her eyes and hear it in her voice when she told me all about last night at breakfast. I know she loves him. And I think she could forgive him if he wouldn't keep secrets from her anymore once this war has ended.

He's kind to her. He wants her. And I know she wants him too. The only thing that stands in the way are the names the reporter keeps talking about on the television and the fact that Addison now knows Daniel has a hand in that tragedy.

"I was having nightmares before, so maybe that's why?" I surmise and then shrug, pretending like the vision of my mother didn't just take over my mind this second. I glance at Eli, still standing there a few feet away, looking straight ahead and waiting for me. Focusing on him and not on where my thoughts were going.

"Nightmares?" she asks, and I only nod as I swallow down the memory.

"I'm sorry," Addie says, and I wish she didn't. I don't need more sympathy. Sympathy doesn't do shit.

"It's been a while since I've had them." I know I have Carter to thank for that. "Anyway, there's a vial that was in my bag in the drawer of my nightstand. If you want it," I offer her, and she gives me a small smile.

"Thanks," she tells me in a way that I know she's truly grateful as she yawns and then stands graciously.

"Sleep well, Fiery Priestess," I tell her with a small smile and watch as she picks up the cards off the floor and puts them on the coffee table.

"You too, Ria," she tells me and uses the nickname only two other people have used for me all my life. She doesn't see how my face blanches, but I'm able to fix it in time before she looks up at me with a sweet smile. "Ria, the card reader," she adds to the nickname and smiles.

I leave without saying goodbye, but it doesn't escape me that Eli keeps looking at me curiously because he saw how I reacted. Eli sees everything.

* * *

TONIGHT FEELS darker than the night before. Maybe because there aren't any stars out, or maybe it's just my perception. Either way, it's pitch fucking black.

It's colder too and as I huddle into the jacket, I find myself walking faster to get to the corner store that I saw a few shops down last night.

"You're quiet," Eli comments as the wind blows and my hair whips around my face. His faint accent comes through more now than I've heard before. I almost ask him about it, but my mind is spinning over the king of wands and who it could be. I always look too much into my cards... and that reading wasn't even mine.

"I'm always quiet," I answer him and when he gives

me this charming, perfect smile, I nearly smile too. I watch him as he looks up to a house in the middle of the street and I know to wait when he does that, just like last night, so I do. Shoving my hands in my pockets, I breathe out and let the cool air flow over me, calming my anxiety.

"I had a girlfriend once who liked those cards. The reading ones."

"Tarot cards," I tell him as he rocks on his heels, still waiting at the edge of the street.

"Yeah, she liked to read mine, one a day, and tell me how my day was going to go."

A simper pulls at my lips. "Was she right?" I ask him, and he huffs a laugh while shaking his head.

"She was so wrong that I could almost guarantee the opposite of whatever she said was actually going to happen."

"They're really just to get you thinking," I tell him and ask, "Are you still together?"

He shakes his head and says, "She was fucking crazy." A genuine laugh bubbles in my chest at the expression on his face, and for the first time today, I feel warmth flow through me. I feel real for a moment... until the reality of everything going on hits me hard in the center of my chest.

"You're good at distractions," I say while pulling my hair to the side as another breeze comes by. As I do, the sound of a car driving a street or two down catches my attention. "Thank you for that," I add with as much sincerity as I can.

"I'm sorry you're in the middle of this," Eli offers me and all I can do is force a fake smile to my lips.

His earpiece buzzes with someone's voice and I step forward, ready to continue but his large forearm blocks me. "We're going back." His voice is stern and offers no negotiation.

"What's wrong?" I ask him feeling my heart race, and counting how many streets we've walked down. Three. It's right around the corner and the safe house is only three streets away.

I can barely breathe as he tells me, "Now," ignoring my question and wrapping his arm around my waist to quicken my steps.

I can't keep up with his fast pace as my body catches fire with fear.

As the muted voices come through his earpiece again, I peek up at him, trying to listen, wanting to know what's going on.

There was no one on the streets. Not a soul. What the hell happened?

Headlights come from my right. And between it all--the voices, the panic, the lights--I stumble, falling to the ground like a fool.

My knees and palms both hit a lawn hard as Eli tries to pull me along, cutting through the yard to head straight to the house, but I struggle to push him off of me, so I can stand up. I just want to stand up but he's hurting me as he tries to pull me up.

The parked car to my right roars to life, its engine

turning and the sound filling the night just as I hear guns firing.

Bang! Bang! Bang! The guns going off make me scream and my heart leaps into my throat.

"Stay down," Eli grunts as he lies on top of me, covering me, but he doesn't stay there for long. The bullets aren't coming this way; they aren't even close.

I can barely see Eli pull out his gun, the cold metal brushing my shoulder before he fires a shot at the car.

There are so many guns going off. Too many to count and I don't know where they're firing, but it's not at me.

Some hit the car. I can hear them crunch into the metal. It pings and some bullets ricochet. Bullets hit the house Eli was looking at, the brick splintering and chips falling past the porch light as if snow is falling on this cold summer night.

Everything happens in slow motion as I peek up, the back of my head slamming into Eli's chest as he fires at the car again, telling me to stay down, but I won't. I need to know what's going on. I keep low, but I refuse to cover my head and not find out what's going on, so I can prepare myself if I have to.

There are four men in the car. I can see them clearly even though they're dressed in all black and hoodies cover their faces. Two are still firing at the building, rapidly pulling the triggers. Men from the building are firing back. Bullet casings hit the ground and the tinkling distracts me as another round of bullets comes closer to us, aimed at another house with men in those windows firing too. We're only separated from the car by a white picket fence that offers no protection and maybe three feet in a yard of grass.

The other two men who were in the car run as I take in the scene. Both of them run down the street to flee although they turn and fire, hiding behind cars and the brick fence. They're running closer to us.

I don't know the car they came from. I don't know the men, but one of them running falls instantly, screaming in agony and grabbing his leg on the sidewalk, the bright red shining brightly as he's bathed in the streetlight.

Bang.

He's silenced and goes still. My heart races, my pulse thrumming so hard I can barely hear the gunshots anymore.

The smacking of shoes carries down the street louder than the gunshots.

"Stay quiet," Eli tells me, intent on hiding as the fucker who's running tries to get away.

He's going to let him get away.

Anger and rage like I've never felt before war inside of me and it burns. It burns too bright. It burns too hot and I can't stand it.

I don't even know it's my own scream as I rip the gun from Eli unexpectedly and run down the street toward the coward who fired at me and the men protecting me. The coward who hid and waited to attack me. I won't fucking let him run.

I won't let him get away. I fucking refuse.

My feet slam so hard on the ground that I feel the pain spike through my thighs. He's only feet away from me and running faster, but he turns to fire at the building again, he slows and turns and that gives me a chance. With a deep intake of the cold air that pains my lungs, I lunge at him, seeing nothing but red.

His head crashes on the cement sidewalk and I hear his gun fall into the street and sounds like it hits metal... maybe a gutter. I didn't recognize him farther away and I don't know him now that I'm close up either. I don't know who he is other than someone who attacked us.

Even as the metal slams into his skull, I don't hear the gunshots stop. Even as the blood splatters onto my face, the heat of it nothing compared to the raging burn that flows through my own blood, I don't hear Eli yelling for me.

I don't stop, I can't make myself stop pummeling his flesh with the butt of the gun. I can't even see what I'm doing with the tears flowing down my face. I try punching him with the gun held in my hand and the metal clashes against the thin skin over my knuckles. It hurts, I know it does, but that only fuels me to do it again.

The footsteps are loud and they're coming closer, but I can still feel the man beneath me shoving me away. His hands pushing against my chest, my face, anywhere until they stop to cover his face.

I pause for only a second and it's a second too much as he reaches for the gun. Panicking, I lean forward, head-butting him and crashing my forehead against his nose. He screams out, but he doesn't stop.

He's still trying to reach for his gun and so I whip the butt of the gun in my hand down hard against his throat and his hot blood bubbles up from his lips as he coughs.

Strong hands grip my shoulders and then my arms, but I kick out, desperate to connect with the fucker who dared to wage war with men protecting me.

My left shoe hits his chin and his head snaps backward, bashing against the cement. Everything in my mind becomes a fog as Eli holds me close to him, telling me to calm down and dragging me away. All I can see is that man running away, getting away without any consequences while they escort me back, through the yards and straight back to where we came from.

It all happened so fast that I'm still breathing chaotically and shaking when Eli and another man, who helped him rip me away, bring me inside.

"Get her inside." I hear Eli's words, but they're slurred as I struggle to breathe.

The air isn't cold anymore. Nothing is cold. It's all hot and I feel like I'm suffocating.

The second the bright light of the foyer hits me, I shove them away. I don't want to be touched, I can't be touched right now.

I refuse to talk to them, to listen to them telling me to stop and calm down.

Calm down? How can I calm down when this is what my life is?

"I'm tired of taking orders!" is all I can yell out, my voice raw from screaming. The memory of what I've done seeps in slowly as I rock on the floor. I was screaming. I didn't realize it then, but I was screaming.

Every time I swallow, it hurts. My shoulders shudder and Eli tries to comfort me but I shove him away. Backing into the corner of the foyer, I'm only seeing the vision of me running after the man and fighting him.

Time passes slowly.

I steady my breathing and slowly calm down, watching my hands and willing them to stop shaking. There's so much blood on them and I wipe them off on my pants, but that just spreads the blood.

I walk myself to my room, gripping on to the railing to keep me upright. Eli follows but stays a good distance behind. Carefully stripping out of the stained clothes, I step into the hot shower to wash the blood away, although my knuckles are raw and cut. It will take time for those to heal.

Maybe an hour passes, and I spend the entire time in the shower. When I'm clean, I walk downstairs and open the front door to the house to see Eli, the other man, and two others standing guard.

All I want to know is his name. I want the name of that man. I don't know why it matters as much as it does, but I need to know his name.

I know I look foolish with wet hair that clings to my face and pajamas on, but still, I speak up.

"Who is it?" I ask Eli as I stand in the light of the

foyer, and he stays on the other side of the doorway, bathed in darkness. "What's the man's name?"

"We'll find out soon and I'll tell you immediately," he answers me, and it only makes me angrier. How can he not know? It still hurts when I swallow and hurts, even more, when I clench my hands into fists at my side.

"Where is he?" I ask Eli with my teeth clenched, "I'll beat it out of him myself." The rage I feel is unjustified and I know I'm out of control and crossing a line, but I don't care about boundaries anymore. Not when everyone else crosses them.

The silence is only broken by the chirp of crickets from beyond the yard. There are three men in front of me and no one answers me.

I can hear Eli swallow as the other men stare at me, and still, no one answers.

"Where is he?" I repeat myself, ready to tell them to go fuck themselves if they refuse to tell me. I don't care what Carter ordered. I don't care if I'm their enemy or they think I'm just being babysat. "I need to know his name!"

"He's dead, Aria." Eli's voice is softer than I expected, and I have to take in a shuddering breath. His gaze is assessing, but comforting. "He died."

My eyes flicker over his and then dart to the other men. "Who killed him?" My voice is full of both shock and remorse for speaking to him like that, along with everything else. As time moves forward, I seem to come down, to ground myself again. As if blinking finally removed the red rage that blinded me.

One man steps to the side, another whispers something on the porch, but Eli's voice brings my attention back to him.

He answers me, "You did."

CHAPTER 17

Carter

"Do you think she'll be a problem?" Jase asks me in low tones as he stares across the bar at the brunette. She stands out in the club full of women dressed in tight shirts and short skirts.

Dressed in jeans with rips in the knees and a loose black tank top designed for comfort, she doesn't belong here. More than that, she's slamming her hands against the bar and screaming across the counter at both the men working tonight.

"She's not why we're here," I remind him. "Let the bartender handle it," I tell him and walk past the crowds of people, but Jase stays behind a moment longer, staring at the deranged brunette.

All I care about are the men in the back room right

now. Men who lost a family member tonight. Two of our guys were shot in the back while they were out on their runs to collect. The fucked-up part is that they were on the most southern portion of our turf. So, some fucker came into our territory, hid low, and shot them in broad daylight. Some fucker named Charles Banner who's now buried in a shallow grave thanks to Cason.

It doesn't bring the men back though. Death is final.

When I walk up to the back doors, Jared opens them immediately and the hushed voices of the six men inside are silenced. I can hear Jase pick up his pace behind me and come in before the doors close, quieting the music of the club.

Around the table, all six men have drinks in front of them, two of them with shots untouched. Cigarettes are lit and one of the guys takes the last puff before putting out the butt. As he blows out the smoke, the rest of the five greet me and then he follows.

The metal chair legs drag on the floor as Jared pulls out seats for both Jase and me and then goes back to his position to guard the doors.

"James and Logan." I swallow thickly after I look both men in the eyes. The youngest one, James, lost his brother and his eyes are still bloodshot. He can't stop himself from crying as I tell him, "I'm sorry." Logan lost his cousin, his only cousin and he's the one who brought him in. I can see the look of regret on his face and there's nothing I can do to take that back.

The other four men all lost a close friend.

Only two men have died tonight on our side, and we took out nearly thirty of Talvery's crew. It doesn't make the losses any easier to take. Not for the six men sitting here.

"What happened was a tragedy and one that needs to be rectified."

"I thought they said you got him?" A kid with a deep scar down the left side of his face and blonde hair speaks up. His lips stay parted as he stares at me with wide eyes. "They said he's dead."

"The asshole who stole the lives of my men?" I question him, bringing my hand to my chest. "The one who pulled the trigger was shot in the back of the head and buried in the back of the construction site off the highway. Tomorrow cement will cover him, and his name will be forgotten." I pause as the kid nods. His name escapes me, and I look around at the other four. I know three of them and then I come back to the blonde. Matthew. That's right. "Matthew?" I call him out and he nods again, bringing his gaze up from where it was focused on the table.

"You can call me Matty." He brightens for a moment, and it's then that I remember one of the guys who died was his neighbor. They grew up together.

"How old are you?"

"Just turned twenty-two," he tells me, and I turn around and motion for Jared to come closer. "Get him as many drinks as he wants all week. A birthday should be celebrated. Every day alive should be celebrated."

"Thank you, Boss," Matty tells me and I shake my head, not wanting any gratitude.

"The man who's responsible for your brother's death," I look to James and then to Logan as I continue, "and your cousin's death, Nicholas Talvery, will die the second I have a chance to end his life."

I pause as the memories of how he tried to kill me, how sneaky the fucker is, spring to mind. Always preparing and setting up his men to blindside the unsuspecting, like my brothers, when we were only kids. "No one," my voice hardens, "will take from us without having consequences."

My heart races as I look the two men on my right in the eyes. "He killed your family and I'll have his head for it."

"To the end of Talvery," Matty raises the shot glass in his hand and the other men do the same.

Talvery.

I'm numb as they throw back the shots and commiserate together.

"To the end of this war," Jase speaks up, grabbing another shot glass and filling his and then the others.

The guy's spirit picks up, although Logan still looks lost. James pats him on the back as Logan hunches over, shaking his head and crying again.

This war is useless. A fight between two men, Romano and Talvery, who already have enough. Greedy, selfish men who will risk lives to hurt the other.

And I supported it.

And Jase wants more of it.

And Aria lies in the middle of all of it.

"If you need anything, you know who to call," I hear Jase speak quietly to the two men on the right and then he stands, and I do the same. Buttoning my jacket and taking a good look at each of the men sitting there.

None of them blame me and that's the worst part of it. I'm bitter knowing they don't blame me when they should. I brought them into this.

For her.

I agreed to this… for her.

The sound of Jase walking ahead of me is all I can follow as I feel like I'm suffocating. Maybe that's how I'll die. I'll choke on every fucked-up decision I ever made.

I feel my phone vibrate in my pocket. It's been going off since the bar, but I wanted to get in and out and give the men the respect they deserve. That's the least I could do.

Feeling it go off again as we step out into the night air and wait for the car to come around, brings on the restlessness and unease that hasn't left me since I left Aria alone on the bed.

"That brunette's gone," Jase comments, leaning against a post by the curb that details all the drink deals inside.

As I pull out my phone, I glance at his profile and for a moment I see the look of loss in his eyes. He's looking out into the parking lot and past it to the busy street. I know what he's thinking about. I know what that look means.

"You all right?" I ask him, and he clears his throat, coughing into his fist and kicking off the post.

"Yeah," he answers and runs his hand down the back of his neck. "I just can't believe Talvery would waste a man like that. Did he really think he'd get out alive?" he questions, and I wonder if he's telling me the truth about what he was thinking, or if I was right.

The rumble of the engine and the soothing sound of my car pulling up grabs our attention and saves me from asking him and prying.

It's not until I walk around and open the door that I check my phone and see the missed calls and texts. Eli never texts, and he knows not to.

A's SAFE *and sound but shit happened. Call me when you can.*

IT's the only text I've ever received from him. And I read it over and over, not breathing.

She's safe. Anxiety creeps up and doesn't leave me, forcing me to unbutton my collar as I walk around the other side and tell Jase to get out and drive. My hand slams on the roof when he doesn't move fast enough. "You drive!" I scream at him and feel raw fear at the back of my throat.

She's safe.

"What's wrong?" He doesn't object but stares at me the entire time he moves around to the other side.

With the key in the ignition, he sits there staring at me while Eli's phone rings.

"Come on," I grit out.

"What's wrong?" he asks again.

"Drive to the safe house," I yell at him, irritated by Eli not answering and pissed off that I'm here and not with Aria. But more than anything I'm scared that something happened to her. It's been nearly forty minutes since he called.

The ringing stops and it goes to his voicemail. *Motherfucker*. I lean forward, my palms on the dash and try to calm the fuck down. *She's safe*.

"Tell me again how we should take on more when this shit is out of hand," I mutter to Jase as he pulls up to a stop sign.

"What happened?" he asks again, incredulity in his voice. I stare at my brother, not knowing what to say because I don't fucking know. I need to know.

"She's safe," I say out loud but it's more of a reminder to myself and Jase asks, "Aria?"

As I nod my head, the phone rings in my hand.

"Eli," I answer quickly, feeling my pulse throb harder.

"We have a problem," he tells me as Jase makes a right and then stops at the light. He's staring at me instead of watching the road.

"Four men on First Street took a shot at our crew. They knew where they were and went for the two stations at the end of the security block. Only one of our guys took a shot, he's with the doc now and he'll be fine."

One breath out, a deep, low breath and I swallow the spiked knot of fear. *She's fine*, I remind myself. My eyes close and my head falls against the headrest.

My heart is thudding, rather than beating.

"Whose men?" I ask him, and he answers, "Not Romano or Talvery."

My jaw clenches, as does my fist. Fucking great. That's the last thing I need right now. Another asshole fucking with me.

"Anything else?" I ask him, opening my eyes and staring at the cabin of the car. The red and white lights from outside dance on the ceiling as he speaks. "All four men are dead, but they were known to hang out with the man who tried to take Addison. The one Daniel killed back when he was checking out Iron Heart. Men for hire. And Carter," he pauses and so does the beat in my chest. I know it has to do with Aria. I can feel it. "I was with Aria at the time. She was there."

I can't swallow. I try, but I can't. There's something in the way and I can't breathe.

"She's okay. But she was there, and she fucked up one of the guys."

My gaze shifts to Jase, who's asking me what's going on. I can only stare at him as I question Eli, "What do you mean, she fucked one of them up? You're supposed to protect her!" The rage is minuscule compared to everything else I feel. The shock and fear that she was there, the relief that she's safe and fine. The pride that she fought alongside my men.

I can hear him huff and it sounds like he switches ears to tell me, "She killed a guy. She got away from me, chased him down the street and beat the piss out of him."

My Aria. My songbird.

"I'll remember that the next time she lets me off with a warning," I say softly, imagining it happening but I can't. I can't see it.

"Is she upset?" I ask him, knowing she will be. I yearn for a time when she's happy again. When this is all over and she looks at me the way she did before.

"She's not handling it well, but she honestly wasn't doing that good before it went down."

"Anything else I should know?" I ask him as I see the sign for Hill Road and Jase turns the corner, not slowing down. The tires squeal as Eli tells me that's it.

"I'll be there in a minute. Gather the guys, I want to go over everything and see the footage."

CHAPTER 18

Aria

I'VE KILLED TWO MEN, yet I don't feel sorry.

Staring at myself in the mirror as I brush out my hair, I don't feel sorry at all. I'm empty inside, and there's no sense of remorse; I don't even have anger left. Nothing. I feel nothing for the man I killed tonight. I remember his wide eyes full of fear. I can feel his hands on me, pushing me away. I can feel the thud of the gun hitting my skin over and over as it crashed into him.

And yet, I feel nothing.

Even Stephan. Thinking of him makes me feel nothing at all.

The hairbrush tugs as I pull it through a knot, and I take my time to carefully brush it away.

I think I must be sick. It can't be normal to feel nothing at all when hours ago I killed a man. My eyes drift to the mirror and I stare at the woman I've become. I look the same as before. The same eyes, my mother's eyes. The same everything as months ago.

But I'm not that girl anymore. The problem is, I don't know who I am.

Without Carter... suddenly the emotions flood back, and I have to slam the brush down on the vanity. It's an antique piece of furniture and I stare at the weathered wood top wishing it would give me answers and take this pain away.

He told me I would always be his and it gave me a freedom. But that freedom scares me now that he left me. I don't think he'll ever take me back and it leaves me feeling hollow inside. There's nothing remaining but the ache of him not loving me.

I suck in a breath, knowing I need to accept it and think about where I'll go and who I'll be once this week and this war are over.

All I know for certain is that I'll be alone. And that sounds like the worst thing in the world when you're empty inside.

I don't want to be alone.

The knock at the bedroom door startles me and I nearly jump in my seat. "Come in," I call out, opening the drawer to the vanity and placing the hairbrush inside.

My gaze catches the phone still sitting on the vanity. A phone that's been silent all day and all night.

What's the point of giving it to me if he had no intention of using it?

It works both ways. I know I could call him. But I'd rather let the tension sever what's left between Carter and me. It's best to let it slip away so when my time's up here, it'll be easier to walk away.

"You're not in bed yet?" Addison's soft voice carries into the room.

"Can't sleep," I tell her, not looking her in her eyes. I may not feel sorry for what I did, but I still don't want Addison to know. I don't want her to look at me and see the heartless killer I can be.

"I know the feeling," she sighs and makes her way to my bed. Sitting on the end of it, she pulls her knees up and pushes her heels into the mattress. "I wanted to check on you," she tells me hesitantly. Her voice is careful, considerate, but her eyes dart from her painted toenails to where I'm sitting as if she doesn't know if what she has to say should be said.

My pulse flutters. Maybe she already knows.

"What's up?" I ask her, refusing to let the anxiety take over. I am who I am. I've done what I've done. If she doesn't understand that, there's nothing I can do about it. I can't take back what's been done.

"Eli said you needed a little space earlier when I came down." I thought I heard something outside... I decided not to sleep and just shower, but when I got out it sounded like..." She picks at the fresh polish on her nails and peeks at me. "He said you were in the shower but to give you some space because you didn't seem like yourself?" she questions me, not trusting what Eli said to be true.

Swallowing thickly, I nod and then wet my lips. "There was an incident on the way to the corner store, but it's okay." I shrug my shoulders and turn back to the vanity, picking up the phone and holding it up for her to see before dropping it into my lap. "Nothing serious enough for Carter to call and reprimand me," I huff a sarcastic response while rolling my eyes, trying to lighten the truth of what happened.

Glancing at the phone, and then meeting my gaze she asks, "So you're all right?"

"Yeah." My answer is easy and I'm hoping she'll drop it.

"And you and Carter?" she asks and then adds, "If you don't want to talk, that's fine." Her voice is stronger, louder and contains no offense whatsoever. "I know sometimes people like to keep things in."

"I like to talk," I tell her honestly and then feel the tug of a sad smile. "Sometimes." My voice is low and so quiet I'm not sure she heard. "Some things I'd rather not talk about, but even still, I always like to talk about something. And when it comes to Carter..." The emotions swell in my throat, stopping the words from coming easily. "When it comes to Carter, I think maybe the best thing to talk about is how to move on from someone you love when they don't love you."

"I'm sorry." The sympathy in Addison's voice pushes the ache in my chest down to the pit of my stomach.

"It is what it is. He made mistakes, I made mistakes,

but none of it matters anyway. We could never be together. Not being the people we are." The words come out easier and clearer than I imagined they would. Addison's expression remains soft as she searches my gaze for something. I'm not sure what.

"What's going to happen then?" she asks me, breathing in deeply and wrapping her arms around her legs while setting her chin on her knees. Sitting feet away from her at the vanity, I wish I had an answer for her, but all I can think is, "Maybe I'll do what my friend, Addison did once, maybe I'll travel the world."

With a hopeful smile and optimism in my voice, I add, "I'd like to be like her."

Addison's smile is less than joyous as she replies, "I heard she did that because she was afraid." Her lips pull down and she bites down on her bottom lip. "I ran away, Aria. I ran because I couldn't face what was left here."

"Do you regret it?"

"No," she answers in a quick breath and seems to struggle to say something else, so I push her to speak her mind. "Whatever you're thinking," I tell her, "you don't have to hide it from me. I won't judge you."

"I don't regret it, because it all brought me back here and brought me back to Daniel." Her voice cracks and she looks away, back to the closed door of the bedroom.

"So, you and Daniel?" I ask her and keep my weak smile in place, no matter how my gut churns. She's going back to him and I'm going to be alone.

"I love him, Ria," she tells me softly, not realizing how she's pulling at every emotion inside of me.

"I know you do," I somehow, some way, speak the truth without letting on how much pain my heart is in. I'll lose Carter because I'm not the woman he needs. And I'll lose Addison because Daniel will never let her go and she'll never let him go either. Even if that means she'll turn a blind eye to the things he does.

As if reading my mind, she tells me, "I don't agree with what he does sometimes, but I know he has his reasons. And I'm so sorry, Aria," she apologizes, and I cut her off, waving my hand in the air recklessly.

"Stop it. Don't apologize. You get it now, don't you?" I ask her, feeling winded by the question. By the idea that with her answer, she still may not understand this complicated mess of pain and love that Carter and I make together.

"I don't agree with it," she tells me with sad eyes, but she doesn't deny that she understands why.

"You don't have to," I tell her and then wipe the sleep from my eyes. "It's weird, but it makes me feel better knowing you understand. Even if it's still not..." Right. Right is the word I nearly say, but it can't be the correct word. Because I don't care how wrong what we had was, it was right for me. It was right for me.

And I refuse to call what we had wrong.

"Does it upset you that I still love Daniel?" she asks me, and I shake my head no.

"If I were you, I'd love him too. He'll fight for you till the day he dies." I almost get choked up, knowing

Daniel would do just that. While Carter won't even tell me he loves me. It shouldn't matter to me as much as it does. But not hearing those words from him... it's killed a part of me that I don't think will ever breathe again.

A yawn creeps up and the exhaustion and weight from everything that happened today, every loss, every failure, makes me crave sleep.

I could sleep forever if sleep would take away this pain.

"I didn't mean to get into all that," Addie tells me, moving off the bed and brushing her hair to the side. She runs her fingers through her hair as she tells me, "I didn't sleep earlier, and I was wondering if you had that vial?"

Getting up from the vanity, I leave the phone on the worn wood top and make my way to the dresser. It's so quiet tonight, it's only as I open up the dresser drawer and hear the pull that I realize I can't hear the crickets. There have been crickets the last two nights, so loud that I had to pretend they were singing me a lullaby in order to sleep.

With the vial in my one hand, I shut the drawer with a hard thud and peek out of the window.

"It's so dark tonight, isn't it?" I ask Addison, the thin curtain grazing my fingers before I pull it back and face her.

"It is. Maybe tomorrow we'll see the stars," she says with a hint of a smile on her lips.

"Sweet dreams." The words slip from me as I pass the vial to her and she tells me goodnight.

As she leaves me alone in the quiet, dark room, I can't help but feel like it's the last night I'll tell her goodnight. Something inside of me, something that chills every inch of me is certain of it.

The covers rustle as I pull them back and climb into bed. I pull them closer to me, all the way up to my neck and stare at the glass knob on the door praying sleep will take me, but the nerves inside of me crawl in my stomach, in a slinking way that makes me feel sick and no matter how tightly I hold the covers, I'm freezing cold. My toes especially.

I almost get up to put socks on, almost. But I can't. A childish fear and feeling deep in my soul wants me to stay right where I am and I listen to that fear, I obey it.

Until my tired eyes burn and the darkness slips in.

Just as I close my eyes, feeling the respite of sleep flow over every inch of me, I think I hear the door open, but when I open my eyes, it's closed. There's no one here.

It's only the darkness and quietness... the signs of loneliness that lie with me tonight.

THE SCREAMS from Addison rip me from my dreamless sleep. My heart pounds against my ribcage as I hear her scream again.

The clock on the dresser blinks at me; hours have passed, and I must have fallen asleep.

My legs feel heavy as I fight with the covers to move fast enough, to get out and go to Addie.

Heaving in a breath I make it halfway to the door before it bursts open. Addie's eyes are wide, her face pale and her hair a messy halo around her head.

"Aria," she cries out my name, pulling me hard into her, so hard it knocks what little breath is in my lungs out of me, but the way she trembles, the way her nails dig into me, I know something's wrong.

"He was here," she whispers in a voice drenched in terror. "I felt him," she whimpers, pulling away from me to close my bedroom door.

As she backs away from me, she almost bumps into me and startles when I carefully take her hand.

Her fear is contagious, and I struggle to remain calm but without any idea of what she's talking about, I have to ask her, "Who? Who was here?"

"Tyler," she tells me and then tears leak from her eyes. She doesn't blink, she stares at me, willing me to believe her as the tears freefall and cradle her cheeks. "Tyler... it felt so real. He was there, Aria. I felt him."

Goosebumps travel over every inch of me and the same coldness that pricked the back of my neck when I saw the king of wands lingers there once again.

"Tyler?" I question her, knowing Tyler's the fifth Cross brother. The youngest. The one who died.

"It was so real," she tells me as she grabs my wrists hard. Too hard. Although it hurts, I don't pull away; I can't. "He's angry," she says, and her words are hoarse and hushed. The intense look in her eyes refuses to let me feel anything but the sincerity and desperation in her words.

Rushing her words, she tells me, "At first, he only held me and I swear I felt him. I could feel him holding me so tightly." She releases me to cover her eyes as she falls to her knees crying harder and harder, but she doesn't stop telling me what happened.

"He held me and told me he still loves me. He said it's okay to love Daniel. He still loves me, and he'll stay with me. But Aria," she finally looks back up to me, with red-rimmed eyes, "he's angry we left. He was never mad. Tyler never got angry and he said we need to go back. He grabbed my arms. He made me promise." She gasps for breath as she grips her own arms, still on her knees and shaking with fear.

My own legs are weak as I lower myself to her eye level. My knees hit the cold hardwood floor. Gripping her shoulders softly, I wait for her to look me in the eyes.

"It was a dream," I tell her, and she shakes her head.

"It was so real."

"The drug," I try to tell her, but she shakes her head harder, her hair viciously flailing around her shoulders.

"He told me to tell you something." Blinking away the tears, she sniffles and tells me, "He said to hold him as tight as you can, or he'll die." My blood turns to ice as I stare into her eyes.

I remember the terror I had. It was only a dream.

It's only a dream. But I don't know how to convince her.

"He told me to leave and I have to," she tells me in a whisper of a breath. "I have to go back." The remorse in the air between us is palpable. And my heart sinks lower.

I don't say a word, I only grip her close to me, squeezing her until the sound of the bedroom door flinging open startles both of us.

My stomach's still in my throat when I see Eli in the doorway, his figure black and silhouetted by the light from the hall.

"I heard screaming and came up to your room," he breathes heavily and then steps in, a look of relief settling over his face. "When I got there, it was empty. You scared the shit out of me, Addison," Eli's accent is thick as he runs his hand over his face, sleep and worry both evident in his bloodshot eyes.

Addison doesn't let go of me, she doesn't move. All she does is look up at him in silence.

"Are you all right?" he asks her, and she shakes her head no.

Her voice croaks when she starts to tell him but then looks at me, "I want to go…"

She holds my gaze and I offer her a small smile, squeezing her hand and sitting back on my heels to tell her, "Go."

"What's going on?" Eli asks and Addison hugs me tight. The tears don't stop when she whispers, "Come with me please."

The idea of going back to Carter…

"He doesn't love me," is all I can tell her, feeling the

last petal wither and die inside of me. "There's nothing for me there."

Her gaze doesn't leave mine. Even as Eli walks closer to us, towering over us and waiting for an answer.

"Tomorrow," she whispers and then hugs me one last time. I can feel her tears on my shoulder and I promise myself to remember this. We'll share a friendship forever, even if we never see each other again.

She breaks the hug before I'm ready to let go, standing and smoothing her nightgown out before wiping the tears under her eyes.

Rubbing her arm and looking sheepish, she tells Eli, "I don't want to sleep."

She walks past him before he can say anything else, slipping into the yellow light pouring from the doorway and going right rather than left, heading to the kitchen, away from her bedroom.

"Is she okay?" Eli asks me in a tone suggesting he truly needs to know; he's genuinely concerned for her.

I feel the ache deep in my body as I stand up on shaky legs, still cold, still tired, and in the depths of my bones, scared. I don't like what terrors that drug brings.

Hold him as tight as you can, or he'll die.

A chill flows over my skin and I look Eli in the eyes to tell him, "She just had a nightmare. It was only a nightmare."

He doesn't speak for a moment and I peek over my

shoulder to check the time, it's past three and I just want a few hours of sleep.

"You should stay with her," I offer him, wanting to be alone and his forehead pinches with a question he doesn't voice.

He stands there a second longer than I'd like, so I look to the door pointedly and then back to him.

"I can never get a good read on you," Eli says and almost turns from me to leave, but I stop him.

"What does that mean?"

"I don't know where you stand and that makes you..."

"It makes me what?" I press him to continue, although there's a threat in the way I say it. The days of him protecting me are few. I know where I'll stand when my father's dead. He's not my friend. I'm smart enough to know that.

"It makes you dangerous. It makes me not trust you because I don't know who you stand for or against."

"I stand for a lot of people. The only ones I stand against are the ones who get in my way." Walking him to the door, I look him in the eyes and tell him, "Remember that," before closing the door and trying to shake off the sick, empty feeling that grows inside of me.

CHAPTER 19

Carter

LEANING against the railing at the bottom of the stairs, I keep hearing her say the lie.

He doesn't love me.

It's a lie to me, but maybe she truly believes it.

"She certainly has a way about her," Eli mutters as he pinches the bridge of his nose and slowly sits at the bottom of the stairs.

"That's one way to put it." My expression is unmoving, and I can't control the scowl. Swallowing the knot in my throat is painful.

"I'm fucking tired," he mutters, and I tell him to go to bed then.

"You staying here?" he asks and I nod. I can't fucking move after hearing her say that. Addison's scream woke me up, but she was faster than I was. I couldn't hear everything, but I got the gist of it: Addison wants to go back, and Aria doesn't.

My heart feels like it's been stomped on, driven over by a tank, and then left for scraps in the dirty gutter.

"I don't know what to do with her," I speak out loud, not liking where my thoughts are going. I want her back in the cell. The core of my soul is screaming at me to put her there. She'll be safe, and she'll forgive me with time. She has to.

"You don't trust her?" he asks and peers up at me and waits for my response.

"I trust that I know what she'll do at this point." I focus on keeping my breathing steady as I listen to Addison upstairs, turning on the faucet in the kitchen. Our voices won't carry well, but if she wanted to, she could hear us.

Eli sighs as he nods his head and runs a hand over his knee.

I hated her father when I was a kid. I hated him for what he did to me. I hated him for letting me go alive. I hated him for what he did to my home and what he tried to do to my brothers.

But I've never hated him more now. Knowing when I put a bullet in his skull, it will kill her. I can already see how she'll look at me. I can feel her nails dig into my skin as she claws at me. I can hear her screaming.

I can already feel his death tearing her away from me. We're hanging on by a single thread and it's because of him. My jaw clenches and I breathe out low and steady, gazing at the molding that lines the stairwell even though I feel Eli's eyes on me.

The silence stretches until I ask him, "What do you think of her?"

"Of Aria?"

With a single nod, I appraise his expression, his body language, his tone. Everything. I can't explain how whenever one of my men is by her or mentions her or her name, I can't explain how anxiety races through me. She's my weakness and I want her to receive nothing but respect for her. Respect and fear.

But given everything that's happened, I don't think anyone knows what to think of her, or what to think of us.

"I think she has the heart of a lover and the temper of a fighter."

"You sound like a true Irishman," I tell him as I huff a response to his answer.

With his asymmetric smirk, he adds, "I wouldn't want to be her enemy and I think the two of you... together, is something that will be feared."

"I wouldn't want to be her enemy either," I say flatly as my stomach knots and my throat gets tighter. But I am. And I always will be.

It's not her that makes it impossible to be together.

It's not me either.

We never had a chance. My gaze falls as I control the numbness that pricks along my skin. I wanted her so badly, I didn't dare look past the desire for her and see the challenges rooted in our very souls.

She may try to love me, but she will always hate me.

"You think you know what she'll do after tomorrow? When they're all dead?" he whispers his question and I nod, feeling the unbearable knot twist even tighter. With the media in an uproar, the cops aren't holding off for much longer. We promised them tomorrow would be the last day we needed them to stay on the west side while we invade from the east. A single bullet to Talvery's head and his factions will fall.

Tomorrow, I'm going to murder her father.

"I think she'll kill me. And I think she'll hate herself for it but feel it was what she needed to do." Eli's gaze falls and my stomach sinks with it. My fingers are so numb I have to clench and relax my hand repeatedly, but it doesn't work to bring life back to it.

"That's ... a..." he fails to respond.

"I'm choosing to be her enemy and to take everything from her. It doesn't matter if she thinks she loves me." The coldness spreads through my chest like ice crackling. "Hate is stronger." I'm surprised by how strong and unforgiving my words are. "She'll want revenge for what I'm going to do. I would want it too."

Eli looks over his shoulder and down the hall, toward Aria's bedroom. "Is that why you haven't gone to her?"

Not trusting myself to speak, I only nod. I can't look her in the eyes and confess how much she means to me, knowing how badly I'm going to hurt her tomorrow.

I won't do that to her. I'm not that cruel.

Bang, bang, bang, bang!

Adrenaline spikes from my toes straight up through my core, freezing my body, then heating it all at once at the sound of guns going off in the distance. My grip on the railing is white-knuckled as Eli stands and speaks clearly into the device on his wrist.

"Where'd they come from?" he asks, and I bring up the surveillance on my phone, all the while listening. It sounded like it came from blocks away and within seconds I can see two cars blocking the road and men leaning out of the windows.

"East," Eli answers but I already know. My heart pumps harder and the blood is fueled by the need to react. To grip the hard metal of a gun in my hand and feel the recoil again my palm after I've pulled the trigger.

I can hear the men screaming from down the street and the bullets firing as my blood heats. Three blocks at most.

A sick smirk begs to pull at my lips. I should have known Talvery would respond recklessly. Sending what's left of his men to their funerals.

THE VOICES RING clear from Eli's earpiece:

Shots fired on Main Street.

Four men on Abbey Road.

Two cars coming up Dorset.

"BLOCK OFF FOURTH STREET; make them come in on foot and don't hold back fire." I give Eli the command and he repeats what I said word for word.

The guns sound off like fireworks and Addison's hard paces carry through the hall. She's soon pounding on Aria's door.

Taking the stairs two by two, I grip the railing and get to her as quickly as I can. My lungs heave as I get to her door. "Stay in there and lock the door. Don't open it for anyone but Eli." All the words stumble out in a single breath and she looks at me for a moment, breathless and hesitant before nodding.

My heart pounds so hard, harder than it has in a long time. It takes me a moment to realize it's due to fear. The very real fear of losing Aria.

"I won't let anything happen to either of you," I say and stare into Addison's eyes and wish they were Aria's. She's just behind the door and I'm drawn to her. My body aches knowing she's so close, but I refuse to go in there.

If I do, I don't know how I'll leave her.

"Stay in her room." I barely get the command out, but Addison hears me. For a moment, I wonder if Aria heard me from behind the door. *My songbird.* The spiked ball grows in my throat as Addison opens the door before retreating behind it. She didn't say a word to me.

Not a single word.

Every muscle in my body is tight and at odds with what I need to do.

The muted sounds of a man screaming, and the continued gunfire is accompanied by Eli yelling out demands on the floor below us.

I try to calm myself and summon the ruthless side of me that will end this as quickly as it started.

The bullets ring out clearly. Automatic weapons that tear through the brick of houses and metal cars. Windows shatter and men yell out.

So, I move.

Quickly and with determination down the stairs.

My stomach clenches and it's the first time I can remember where so much was at stake. Where my thoughts are torn between tactics and emotion.

Between fighting to steal the woman I love and running as fast as I can.

"Bring up all the cars and block off every street," I command Eli while bringing out my phone to text Daniel and tell him where Addison is. The last I heard from him, he was trying to get in touch with Marcus and find out anything he can about the fucker he killed back in Iron Heart.

My heart pounds, and my muscles coil as I listen closely to every word that comes in from the earpiece as I switch to the surveillance screens and watch everything unfold.

I need to move. Standing here is fucking killing me but I have to remind myself that this is war and decoys are common. I won't be fooled like Talvery was.

Three streets on two sides are under attack, two on top of each other to the east and one furthest to the west of this house.

"They hit three streets at once."

"Do we have a count on how many men are firing?" I need numbers. Talvery can't have more than fifty men left.

Eli's earpiece buzzes and it takes everything in me not to rip it out and take it for myself. "It looks to be about thirty."

"They may be distractions, hitting the two sides and leaving the south side untouched. Don't move the men on the south side."

"Yes, sir," Eli answers, speaking into the device.

"Count of our men," Eli barks out the order before relaying what I said. I have fifty men to his thirty. Fifty well-armed and guarded but spread out.

TWO MEN DOWN.

One man down.

We're holding.

I STARE AT MY PHONE, waiting for Daniel to reply, but I get nothing. Where the fuck is he?

"Three total, Boss," Eli's voice is tight as I grip the phone tighter and scream internally for him to tell me where the fuck he is. The cords in his throat tense as he rips the Velcro of his holster, moving it to the side and checking his ammo.

Three men dead.

Three more men dead.

"Kill them all," I grit out, feeling the rage turn incandescent. My head feels light as I take in a deep breath.

"You and Cason stay with the women," I give the command while my phone pings and Jase tells me he's close and coming up the south side and he already told the guards there.

His jaw is hard and clenched, and I know he wants to be out there, but I need him here.

"You two stay here." I harden my voice and look him in the eyes until he nods.

Shoving my phone in my back pocket, I reach for my gun and then move past Eli to the back room where the other weapons are stored as he tells me, "Yes, Boss."

I need men with them who know when to leave.

The back room has shelves of guns and I choose from the racks of metal shining back at me, picking up one and shoving it and the ammunition into the waist of my pants before picking up another.

Talvery's on the outer edge. There's no way he'll get in and this entire ground is a safe house. But every safe house can be broken into. I've done it before. Sebastian knew that when he built this place.

With time ticking, and the bullets still firing every minute, I turn my back on the arsenal and prepare to join my men. I only stop to tell Eli one thing, "The basement has an underground exit. The code is six, fourteen, eight, eight. Repeat it to me."

"Six, fourteen, eight, eight." He's quick to answer, but I can see the defiance in his eyes.

"Don't forget it, and if I--"

"We have enough men," Eli cuts me off and I struggle to hold back the anger. "There's no way--"

"If I tell you to," I say looking him in the eyes as my nostrils flare and my body heats with the need to strike back, "take them and lock the door behind you."

I don't wait for him to answer, although as I turn my back to him and head down the stairs, I hear him say he'll do it. The buzzing in my ears is like white noise as I climb down the stairs. I'm ready with a gun in my right hand as I stare at the front door.

I pray Talvery's here in the flesh and blood, ready to finally pay for all his sins.

"Carter," Eli calls out to me as I reach the front door.

"What?" I snap at him, feeling the rage, the immediacy, the fear even of losing men and protection for Aria and Addison.

"Your estate... He sent men there." Eli visibly swallows as my blood chills.

"My brothers?" I ask him quickly, my breathing coming in short pants. The gun in my hand slips and I grip it tighter, praying and swallowing down my fear.

"Jase said he's coming," I speak as I remember the text and Eli confirms with a brief nod.

"Jase and Declan are together, they're on their way and missed it."

Daniel. My heart beats slow, so slow it's painful. "Three bombs hit the east wing. And another four to the south wing and the garage."

"How many men are dead?" The question comes out without conscious consent, all I can think of is Daniel and the last time I saw him when he told me he had plans with Addison.

"Six currently."

"Where's Daniel?" I ask him, feeling the threat of a pain that can never be soothed brimming inside of me.

"We don't know."

CHAPTER 20

Aria

"FUCK, FUCK," Addison's rocking back and forth on the bed, her legs tucked up under her as the guns continue to fire.

Men shout from the floor below us and farther down the streets outside.

"I've never heard it last for so long," I whisper as I peek out into the black night. I watch as each of the streetlights is hit, one by one, spraying shards of white light before fading into the darkness.

Addison's voice is strained and coated in worry as she asks, "Why would they do that?"

"So they can't see," I tell her.

"But then no one can see."

"It's a risk they decided was worth taking." I feel the numbness flow through my blood.

"Who did it? Who shot them?" she asks me as if I'd know.

Tires squeal in the distance and metal crashes against metal. She cries harder, falling apart and then checks her phone again. She buries her face in her knees, rocking harder.

"We can hide in the closet," she offers although her words are panicked, and I don't know if she means it or not. "We'll put the clothes on top of us," she gasps for breath and rocks again, "they'll open it but not see us. I used to do it when I was younger. They won't see us. They won't see us."

She's losing it. The way she rocks, the rapid rate with which she's talking and the look of terror in her eyes are clear signs. She's fucking losing it.

"We should have left," she croaks with tears in her eyes and the numbness turns to a freezing cold along my skin.

"He told us to leave."

"It was intuition, Addie," I breathe an excuse even as the gunshots sound louder, closer, the violence making its way to the finish line.

"Where's Daniel?" She covers her mouth as she cries again and struggles to breathe.

I don't know what comes over me as I watch her wither away and dissolve into nothing but fear and sorrow, but my hand whips across Addison's face and she stares up at me in shock before slowly moving her hand to cover the bright red mark.

My hand stings and my heart lurches with the fear of hurting her and losing a friend, but I move closer to her, gripping her shoulders and staring into her eyes to tell her, "We will not die like this."

Her chest rises and falls with heavy breathing as she waits for me to tell her more.

"Come on," I say and pull her wrist. "We're leaving," I tell her, but she pulls away.

"He told us to stay here," she breathes and lets her gaze dart between the door and me.

"I don't care what Eli said." The frustration, the anger, the terror, and lack of sleep, it all makes my body feel as if it's on fire and like I'm losing control, but I raise my voice to yell at her, "Come with me!" My dry throat screams in pain as I swallow and tell her, "We need to run."

The gunshots get louder from outside and steal our attention. They're getting closer. My heart pounds in my chest and the sound of the door opening behind me makes both of us scream. Addison's is shrill and so sharp it nearly punctures my eardrum.

Cason's out of breath as he makes his way toward us and says, "We're going to the basement." Addison shakes her head violently, and asks the only question she's been praying to have an answer to, "Where's Daniel?"

The pang in my chest strikes hard and I feel like I'm

suffocating as I pray to know the same, but about Carter.

The phone is silent. My text to him unanswered.

ARE YOU OKAY?

IT'S all I wanted to know. And he didn't answer.

"Basement. Now!" Cason yells just as bullets fly past us. The windows shatter, the small pieces raining over Addison, who covers her head with her arms and drops as far as she can forward onto the bed. I fall instantly, lying flat on the floor as I hold my breath, too afraid to move at all. Her shrill scream fills the room again as bullets ricochet and leave a trail of marks from left to right over the wall and bedroom door.

My eyes reach Cason as he stands up straight. He didn't move. He never had the chance to move. The bullet holes in his chest slowly bleed out, the bright red diffusing and spreading like watercolor paints on canvas.

"No," I breathe, tears pricking my eyes as his hand moves to one of the punctures at the same time as he falls to his knees. "Cason!" I scream out his name and reach for him, but it's useless.

The gunshots have stopped; it was a single string of bullets that clattered across the house. But they return again within seconds. Hitting him again in his neck and head, eyes closed before he falls to the floor.

Addison doesn't scream this time although I can hear her sobs from where I am. Reaching up for her, I pull her down and together we crawl on our stomachs under the bed.

"Daniel," Addison cries his name over and over, her hands clasped as she prays for him to be all right.

I can't breathe. It's so hot and the bullets rain down with no signs of letting up for minutes. More time passes with nothing. No signs of anything and that's when I see the gun on the floor. Cason's gun. As I crawl out, Addison grabs me and yells for me not to leave her. My heart lurches at the sound of a door being kicked in downstairs.

"Shh," I hush her, putting my finger over my lips and then nodding to the gun. With wide eyes, she watches me as I crawl out to get it. The cold beating in my veins picks up as the sound of a man coming up the steps gets louder and louder. The open bedroom door shows his shadow in the hall just as I reach the gun with my fingertips.

The cold metal slips in my grasp and the sound of it sliding across the floor rips my gaze up to the doorway. Without looking, I snatch the gun and Addison pulls me back under the bed.

The gun is heavy, so heavy in my hand. Addison's hands are covering her mouth as a shadow steps into the room. The floor creaks with the man's weight and his black boots are splattered with blood.

I grip the gun with both hands as he takes three agonizingly slow steps closer to Cason's body, right before kicking his shoulder over with his boot to see his face.

Bending down, I get a partial glimpse of the man as he steals Cason's phone from his pocket. The fear is paralyzing. I can't breathe. I can't do anything.

My gaze moves to the vanity and I can see my reflection, but I can see the man's too as he scowls down at Cason's dead body and lifts his gun to his head.

Bang, bang!

The gun goes off and Addison jolts each time, her eyes closed tight and her hands pressing harder against her mouth.

My heart hammers, praying he didn't hear her, but it doesn't matter if he did or not, because the man's eyes reach mine in the mirror. Cold and dark, with wrinkles that show his age. He's in the same black hoodie as the man I killed earlier, and I know this man is not one of my father's men.

The attacks out there, I think they're from my father. But the men who have made it to the safe house... they're not.

He's quicker than me, taking a large stride and grabbing me from under the bed. His grip on my left forearm is paralyzing and I nearly drop the gun. My back scratches against the underside of the wire bedframe and the pain forces a scream from me.

My finger is on the trigger and I can't get it to go off. I pull it again and again.

"The safety." Addison's voice is hoarse, and the words pushed through clenched teeth.

He reaches down with his other hand, grabbing my other wrist and that's when Addison rips the gun from me and fires. The heat from the barrel of the gun singes my skin and I scream from the pain.

Bang! Bang!

She pulls the trigger again and again as my left side falls to the floor with the man's grip nonexistent.

I can hear Addison's gasp and the clunk of the gun as the man's dead white eyes stare back at me.

My hollow chest is gutted as I stare at him and then to the doorway. My heart beats too loudly to hear anything and I have to swallow and blink away the fear to grab the gun Addison dropped and point it at the door.

I lie half under the bed, half out, with a burn scorching my forearm and wait. Time passes quickly, as quickly as my blood races through my veins.

"He's dead," Addison whispers a painful truth. "I killed him," she whispers.

"Shh," I hush her, "Quiet!"

The pounding of my heart slows as I realize the man almost got me and she saved me.

"You saved me," I whisper with tears in my eyes although I stare straight ahead.

"I killed him," she says back in a harsh whisper.

It's only then that I realize it's silent once again. No gunshots. Not from outside and not a sound inside the house.

I listen closely and hear cars outside a few blocks down, but they aren't rushed and the tires don't squeal. Rising slowly, I nearly scream when Addison grabs my ankle.

"Fuck," I barely get out the word over the harsh beat of fear in my chest.

"Is it safe?" Addison asks, and I tell her the truth, "I don't know."

It's hard to contain terror, even when there's no present danger. My gaze doesn't leave the doorway as I crawl to the window. Even as I rise up slowly and pull the curtain ever so softly, I don't dare take my eyes from the doorway for a few minutes longer.

No more gunshots and lights are on inside the houses that were black now. A car passes with its headlights and I see some men I recognize a street down.

"I think it's over," I whisper to her but still crawl to reach her. "Take the gun," I put it in her hand and when she objects I tell her I'm taking the dead man's gun.

"I'm going downstairs." With my words, Addison's eyes go wide and she grips my wrist with a bruising force. My breathing is still unsteady, and my heart doesn't find a normal cadence either.

"I have to make sure it's okay. I'm going to find Eli," I tell her, and the mention of Eli seems to calm her down. Her cheeks are red, and tears still linger in her eyes.

"Stay here," I whisper and put my hand over hers. I squeeze it once before leaving her, crawling past the dead man, and taking his gun with me. I don't stand up until I'm past the door. Blood coats my pajama pants from where I crawled through it. Standing outside the door and staring at the stairwell, I breathe in deeply over and over, trying to calm myself.

Small shards of glass pierce my forearms and I pick them out, wincing as I do. The pain is nothing with all the adrenaline running through me, but still, I'm mesmerized by the bright red and the evidence of what we've just been through.

The moment I close my eyes, a phone rings behind me.

Ring, ring and my heart shudders in my chest. A shuddering as if being brought back to life. "Daniel," Addison's voice rings out clear, the moment I think Carter's name.

My throat goes dry as I swallow and hear her tell him how worried she was.

Carter didn't call.

It's not Carter.

It takes everything in me to step forward. The feeling of loss runs deep in my blood and I struggle to keep it together. One heavy step after another, with the gun in my right hand and my left hand gripping the railing, I walk down the steps quietly, hearing the faint sounds of Addison from the bedroom and nothing else in the house.

I may not have felt anything for the man I killed upstairs, nothing but hate, and less than that for the other man in the same black hoodie who died earlier today, but as I stand over Eli's dead body in the foyer, I cry.

Heavy sobs that bring me to my knees and steal the warmth from my body.

I can't breathe as my trembling fingers touch his throat, searching for a pulse, but finding none.

My feet kick out and I crawl backward, away from his body until my back hits the wall.

Covering my face in the crook of my arm, I can't stop crying.

His life was wasted on mine. Cason's life wasted on mine.

How much death can I be responsible for, before I lose any love I could possibly have for myself?

The opening of the back door, the slamming of the knob into the wall forces me to go silent. I hold my breath and crawl to the other corner as the footsteps quicken.

"Fuck, no," Daniel's voice carries into the foyer as he reaches Eli. "Shit," he breathes the word with true mourning before his heavy footsteps hit the stairs.

"Addison!" he cries out her name as my head hits the wall and my breath comes in staggered, sharp pulls.

The back door is still open, the wind carries through the house and the cool air calls to me like a siren.

I'm numb as I stand and make my way to the door, with trees lining the back of the yard, it's pitch black, but I can see there's no one here.

There's nothing here.

Nothing but the dark and the quiet as I take a single step out. And then another as the cold flows over my skin. And another.

The thoughts of how life has spiraled downward ever since I laid eyes on Carter Cross run through my mind. Or maybe ever since he laid eyes on me. It's hard to know which, really.

The thoughts consume me as I breathe in the cold air.

The thoughts... and then the hard chest that slams my back into it and the large hand that covers my mouth as I scream.

CHAPTER 21

Carter

I RECOGNIZE some of these faces. Men who have stared at me from a distance with hate but didn't have the balls to pull the trigger. I've passed so many of them on street corners as I drove past Carlisle and sometimes into Talvery territory over the years.

Bang!

I've imagined the bullet holes in their foreheads for years.

My blood is ringing with anger as I point the trigger at a man hunched behind the car and waiting with his back to me for one of my men to come into his view. He won't even see it coming. *Bang!*

Declan's iPad shows each of the streets, lined with dead bodies and riddled with bullet holes, broken glass and the shells of bullets that have stolen dozens of lives tonight.

War comes with a hefty cost and it's sickening but it fuels my need for vengeance.

"Four more on Second Street," Declan speaks into his mic.

Jase and I watch him carefully and keep an eye out on each side of the building we're stationed behind. Declan cheats at war, using surveillance that doesn't let a soul hide.

"Straight down from the street sign, head up the right side of the street and get them from the back. They're behind the--"

Shots ring out and I glance at the screen to see each of the four turning around too late. Their guns held in the air, aiming, but too slow to do anything before their bodies drop.

The night air is quiet.

It hasn't been more than thirty minutes since I've left, but the realization of how much time has passed since I've heard a word about Aria sends a tremor of terror rocking through me like a slow wave.

"We still have the two," Jase reminds me and tugs my arm to follow him.

Only two of Talvery's men are left. But he wasn't among them and neither was Nikolai.

The thought reminds me of Aria, crying on the bed as she confessed how she'll never forgive me if I killed them. How easy it would have been for the two of them to have died tonight at the hands of other men.

Swallowing the regret, I check my phone and see Cason's text that they're secured and safe. He sent it only ten minutes ago. *She's safe.* And at this moment, she's still in my grasp. That's all that matters.

I didn't realize I'd been holding my breath until I read that message and then the next, a text from Daniel saying that he was almost to the safe house.

Go straight to them, I text him and then add, *It's over. There's just a message left to send.*

Jase is peeking over my shoulder and his lip twitches as he mutters, "message to send," and then kicks in the back door, a door scarred with bullet holes. It reveals two men on their knees with a row of my men behind them.

"WHAT ARE YOUR NAMES?" My voice bellows in the small room that looks like it was once used for entertainment. A busted bookshelf stands in the back left corner, board games spilling out over the floor and the projector screen straight ahead is littered with small holes.

Nearly every house on this block and the next will be just like this. The people were cleared out two days ago, bribed or threatened to leave, whichever method was more effective.

Jase crouches down in front of one of the two men and says, "If I were you, I'd answer my brother." The man behind him, the one pointing a gun at our captive lets out a single rough laugh and the man next to him follows.

"Fuck you," the old man says. He's on his knees and bent like that makes his stomach look even larger. He's got to be in his forties and as he spits at Jase's feet, the wrinkles on his face tighten. He nearly topples over without being able to put his hands out in front of him; they're cuffed behind his back, just like his friend to the right of him.

Jase stands up and moves to the next man, but when he does, my heart drops and a sick feeling spreads through my veins. "Where'd you get that hoodie?" I ask him and come closer to him, close enough to grab his collar and pull him up to look at his face.

He's younger with beady eyes and thin lips. He doesn't say anything at all, but there's a hint of a smile on his lips like he knows a secret I don't.

"You," my voice comes out harsh as I drop the asshole in the black hoodie and let him fall hard on the ground. He coughs up a laugh and I grab the old man's shirt, fisting it and the back of his head with my other hand.

"What's his name," I grit out the question and shake the old man, repeating myself in a scream that rips up my throat when he doesn't answer. "What's his name!"

"Fuck, I don't know!" The old man looks back at me like I've gone mad as I breathe heavily, my lungs heaving air.

"This one is Talvery," I drop the old man and move

to the one in the hoodie, the one whose eyes are nothing but a well of blackness.

"This one is hired," I speak as I crouch in front of him, feeling my heart race.

"Talvery doesn't need to hire anyone." The old man speaks up until his executioner chambers a round and the click shuts him up.

"Where did you find this one?" I ask the man standing behind him. When I peer up, I see it's Logan.

He looks to his left and then to his right, stuttering to answer.

"Logan," I stand slowly, "Where did this one come from?"

"He was inside the line, shooting at the target, sir," another man speaks up.

"The target?" My heart pounds, but I remind myself that Daniel should be there.

"The safe house," the soldier clarifies.

A cold numbness runs through me as the man in the black hoodie, barely on his knees says, "My partner went in and finished what I started."

I turn to my brother, who's already on his phone. "Where's Daniel?" I ask him as my chest heaves for air. I squeeze the gun harder and when the fucker laughs at me, a deep laugh that chills the very marrow in my bones and fills the room, I whip it across his face, feeling the force of it splinter up my hand.

"Confirmed man dead in the safe house, wearing a black hoodie," Jase's response soothes the fear, bringing my rage down to a simmer.

"He's dead?" I ask Jase to tell me again as relief teases me.

"Addison said Aria shot him."

"She never fails to amaze me." As much as the pride fills me, there's nothing but rage that shows. Anger that they got close to her. To my songbird. They came close enough to hurt her. My fists clench tightly, spreading the thin skin across my knuckles as I breathe in slowly, deeply, seeing nothing but red.

"Daniel came up the south side, where there was less action and he's with Addison now."

I hear Jase's words, I know I do, but they don't register.

This man with the sick smile on his knees in front me, he conspired to hurt her. My stomach churns at the thought of how narrowly Addison and Aria escaped being hurt, or worse.

The first punch to his jaw, I don't even realize came from me. Not even as the skin across my knuckles splitting sends a pain up my arm. Again and again, I land punches across his face, listening to the cracking of bone in the deafening silence that fills the room.

The pulse of my racing blood is all I can hear. That and the sound of the man spitting blood across the floor as I grab him by the collar and roll him on his back to crouch on top of him. With his hands cuffed behind him, his back arches and he tries to roll back to his side, clenching and giving me daggers through his narrowed eyes.

"Who hired you?" I grit out the question and a beat passes, then another. He huffs a breath through his nose and the corners of his lips pick up in an asymmetric grin, displaying a ring of crimson blood around his teeth.

The fingers of my right hand crush his throat, forcing it to the ground and feeling his blood rush beneath my grip as I slam my fist into his face again. His eye is swollen and when I punch him again, I hear his nose crack and watch blood seep around his eyes, making them black although not nearly as black as the depth of his irises.

"How did you get past my men?" I scream the question, bringing my face close to his. The words tear up my throat, grating as they go and leaving a searing pain. All I can see is Aria, surrounded by men in black hoodies and before he can even answer, I slam my head into his, hearing the sickening crunch of his broken bones grinding against one another from the impact.

I have to release him, to get up and walk around him, staring at the man on the ground and picturing Aria standing over another just like him.

They got too close. Too fucking close.

"That one... that one I'd love to answer." I barely make out the words, they're spoken so softly. He coughs up blood, but then rests his head down on the floor, staring up at the ceiling. The man sways, barely coherent, but the smile still wishes to stay on his lips. It falters as he blinks slowly, his consciousness failing him.

Licking my lower lip, I steady my breath and bend down to get closer to him, gripping the back of his head. I grip onto his skull as I tug at his hair and force him to look at me.

"Tell me," I utter the demand gravely and his eyes flash with something. A look of delicious contentment. It's only then I realize how much I've shown him. How much I've shown everyone.

Aria is my everything. She alone has the will to turn me into a madman.

"Tell me," I push out the words through clenched teeth and feel my muscles coil, ready to assault him again, but he answers quickly this time.

"Every exit is an entrance."

My eyes search his, trying to register the meaning of his words. "I don't have time for—"

"Your little underground escape route... it was our way in. My job was easy, get outside and cause a ruckus, so my partner could do his job." He answers my unspoken question and seems to settle, so I grip his hair tighter, not giving him a moment of comfort.

"And what was his job?"

My heart beats faster, knowing they wanted Addison, but unsure of where Aria stands.

"Wouldn't you like to know," he mutters under his breath as his eyes roll into the back of his skull. I shake the fucker, waking him and stare into his cold gaze.

"Tell me." My command comes out low and vicious, my face getting closer to his as the life slips from him.

"I'll tell you one thing. It was only one girl a month ago, but then he upped it to two."

Bastards! My throat closes, and I struggle to stay where I am, my muscles burning to go to her. To Aria and to keep everyone away from her forever. No one will ever get to her. Never!

"Who did?" I don't know how I'm able to ask the question or to stay still as I wait for his answer.

"I'll die before I tell you," he replies, but then his head falls back. He's close to death already. Close, but not quite there yet.

"Logan," I say and raise my voice, but I don't look away from the man in my grasp. He'll soon be dead.

"Sir?" he asks hesitantly from somewhere to my right. I can hear his feet drag again the floor as he comes closer. "Brass knuckles?" I question him and then the sound of other men moving about registers.

"Someone," I say as I stare straight into my victim's icy gaze, "give me brass knuckles."

"Carter!" Jase shouts my name and rips my attention away. The warmth of blood splatters on my forearm and the man coughs in my grasp.

"What?" My question is sneered, pissed off that he would dare interrupt this. "He came after Aria!" I scream so loud; her name reverberates off the walls as I stare at Jase.

My chest rises and falls, my breathing coming in ragged and faster.

"Carter," Jase's voice is low but accompanied by the sound of the man in my grasp speaking at the same time.

"I couldn't wait to get them," he mutters beneath his breath.

"Carter!" My brother screams at me as I slam my fist into his jaw, hearing it crack as it dislocates. It dangles from his face and the sight only fuels me to take out more of my rage on him.

My shoulders are wound tight, needing more of a release as the asshole falls forward and Jase screams my name again. "Carter!"

"I'm not done with him," I grind out the words as I push Jase away from me, refusing to look at him and not the man who dared threaten my Aria. The man rocks on his shoulder, his face deformed and covered in blood. He has to roll forward to keep from choking on it or drowning in his own blood as he struggles to cough it up, but his movements are weak and slow. He's close. Too fucking close. I want him to live to see what true pain really is.

"Sir," Logan's voice is heard as a metal block is placed in my periphery. I've never smiled as sadistic of a smile as I do now.

"Should I do him the favor of killing him?" I ask no one in particular as I crouch in front of him and slip the thumb of my right hand over the brass that covers the knuckles on my left hand.

"Carter!" My gaze narrows as I peer up at my brother who's reaching out for me, reaching his hand out with a look that begs me to listen to him.

I don't take his hand, but I search his expression. He's worried, his eyes a pit of loss and despair. All the heat in my body suddenly feels doused with ice. A chill runs through me as I ask him with the last breath I have, "What?"

I barely register the painful groan the man, still barely alive, utters at my feet.

"What about Aria?" Jase asks me with a look of desperation and I finally hear the other men in the room. The war isn't over, and this place isn't safe now that it's been breached.

"I'm taking her home." I give him the only answer I can. It doesn't matter what she wants; a man got to her and that's unacceptable. Fuck! I grind my teeth and throw the brass knuckles into the torn projector screen when I remember the house was hit.

My body is shaking, vibrating with the need to protect her yet having my options limited. *I will protect her.* The very thought soothes me. She is mine and no one will hurt her. I'll never let anyone close to her again.

"I'll take her wherever I go." I give him my answer in a tone that brooks no further discussion, hiding the agony of what's devouring my every thought, but that doesn't change the look on his face. It doesn't remove an ounce of the fear in his expression.

"Where is she?" Jase asks, and my pulse slows, the

adrenaline leaving me at the very thought of being with Aria tonight. Even if she hates me tomorrow.

"Daniel has her." I feel my brow furrow when I look at him, and everything slows. It slows and the world around us turns to a faded, blurred image. My heart beats once. He was just talking to Daniel. My heart beats again. "He has her," I repeat when Jase does nothing but visibly swallow and the already quiet room goes completely silent.

"No, he doesn't." I see nothing but red and everything turns to white noise as Jase tells me, "Aria's gone."

To Be Continued...

Carter and Aria's story concludes in ENDLESS. Don't miss the conclusion of their gripping story!

HAVEN'T READ Daniel and Addison's story? You don't want to miss out on their heart-wrenching story, Possessive. Keep reading for a sneak peek.

FOLLOW me on BookBub to be the first to know about my sales!

TEXT ALERTS: Text WILLOW to 797979

AND IF YOU'RE on Facebook, join my reader group, Willow Winters' Wildflowers for special updates and lots of fun!

KEEP READING at the very end for a preview of my *USA Today* Bestseller, Something to Remember. Or you can start reading today for FREE!

W WINTERS READING ORDER

Sinful Obsessions Series:
It's Our Secret
Little Liar
Possessive
Merciless

Standalone Novels:
Broken
Forget Me Not

Sins and Secrets Duets:
Imperfect (Imperfect Duet book 1)
Unforgiven (Imperfect Duet book 2)

Damaged (Damaged Duet book 1)
Scarred (Damaged Duet book 2)

Happy reading and best wishes,
W Winters xx

SNEAK PEEK OF
POSSESSIVE

From *USA Today* bestselling author W Winters comes an emotionally gripping, standalone, contemporary romance.

It was never love with Daniel and I never thought it would be.

It was only lust from a distance.

Unrequited love maybe.

He's a man I could never have, for so many reasons.

That didn't stop my heart from beating wildly when his eyes pierced through me.

It only slowed back down when he'd look away, making me feel so damn unworthy and reminding me that he would never be mine.

Years have passed and one look at him brings it all back.

But time changes everything.

There's a heat in his eyes I recognize from so long ago, a tension between us I thought was one-sided.

"Tell me you want it." His rough voice cuts through the night and I can't resist.

That's where my story really begins.

Possessive is an emotional, gripping story. Filled with heartache, guilt and longing! Possessive will take you on a journey of obsession and jealousy...it's emotional, raw and captivating. - **Beyond The Covers Blog**

PREFACE

Addison

*I*t's easy to smile around Tyler.

It's how he got me. We were in tenth-grade calculus, and he made some stupid joke about angles. I don't even remember what it was. Something about never discussing infinity with a mathematician because you'll never hear the end of it. He's a cute dork with his jokes. He knows some dirty ones too.

A year later and he still makes me smile. Even when we're fighting. He says he just wants to see me smile. How could I leave when I believe him with everything in me?

My friend's grandmother told me once to fall in love with someone who loves you just a little more.

Even as my shoulders shake with a small laugh and he leans forward nipping my neck, I know that I'll never really love Tyler the way he loves me.

And it makes me ashamed. Truly.

I'm still laughing when the bedroom door creaks open. Tyler plants a small kiss on my shoulder. It's not an open-mouth kiss, but still, it leaves a trace on my skin and sends a warmth through my body. It's only momentary though.

The cool air passes between the two of us, as Tyler leans back and smiles broadly at his brother.

I may be seated on my boyfriend's lap, but the way Daniel looks at me makes me feel alone. His eyes pierce through me. With a sharpness that makes me afraid to move. Afraid to breathe even.

I don't know why he does this to me.

He makes me hot and cold at the same time. It's like I've disappointed him simply by being here. As if he doesn't like me. Yet, there's something else.

Something that's forbidden.

It creeps up on me whenever I hear Daniel's rough voice; whenever I catch him watching Tyler and me. It's like I've been caught cheating, which makes no sense at all. I don't belong to Daniel, no matter how much that idea haunts my dreams.

He's almost twenty and I'm only sixteen. And more importantly, he's Tyler's brother.

It's all in my head. I tell myself over and over again that the electricity between us is something I've made up. That my body doesn't burn for Daniel. That my soul doesn't ache for him to rip me away and punish me for daring to let his brother touch me.

It's only when Tyler says something to him, that Daniel turns to look at him, tossing something down beside us.

Tyler's oblivious to everything happening. And suddenly, I can breathe again.

MY EYELIDS FLUTTER OPEN, my body hot under the stifling blankets. I don't react to the memory in my dreams anymore. Not at first. It sinks in slowly. The recognition of what that day would lead to getting heavier in my heart with each second that passes. Like a wave crashing on the shore, but it's taking its time. Threatening as it approaches.

It was years ago, but the memory stays.

The feeling of betrayal, for fantasizing about Tyler's older brother.

The heartache from knowing what happened only three weeks after that night.

The desire and desperation to go back to that point and beg Tyler to never come looking for me.

All of those needs stir into a deadly concoction in the pit of my stomach. It's been years since I've been tormented by the memories of Tyler and what we had. And by the memories of Daniel and what never was.

Years have passed.

But it all comes back now that Daniel's back.

CHAPTER 1

Addison
The night before

I LOVE THIS BAR. Iron Heart Brewery. It's nestled in the center of the city and located at the corner of this street. The town itself has history. Hints of the old cobblestone streets peek through the torn asphalt and all the signs here are worn and faded, decorated with weathered paint. I can't help but to be drawn here.

And with the varied memorabilia lining the walls, from signed knickknacks to old glass bottles of liquor, this place is flooded with a welcoming warmth. It's a quiet bar with all local and draft beers a few blocks away from the chaos of campus. So it's just right for me.

"Make up your mind?"

My body jolts at the sudden question. It only gets me a rough laugh from the tall man on my left, the bartender who spooked me. A grey shirt with the brewery logo on it fits the man well, forming to his muscular shoulders. With a bit of stubble and a charming smirk, he's not bad looking. And at that thought, my cheeks heat with a blush.

I could see us making out behind the bar; I can even hear the bottles clinking as we crash against the wall in a moment of passion. But that's where it would end for me. No hot and dirty sex on the hard floor. No taking him back to my barely furnished apartment.

I roll my eyes at the thought and blow a strand of hair away from my face as I meet his gaze.

I'm sure he flirts with everyone. But it doesn't make it any less fun for the moment.

"Whatever your favorite is," I tell him sheepishly. "I'm not picky." I have to press my lips together and hold back my smile when he widens his and nods.

"You new to town?" he asks me.

I shrug and have to slide the strap to my tank top back up onto my shoulder. Before I can answer, the door to the brewery and bar swings open, bringing in the sounds of the nightlife with it. It closes after two more customers leave. Looking over my shoulder through the large glass door at the front, I can see them heading out. The woman is leaning heavily against a strong man who's obviously her significant other.

Giving the bartender my attention again, I'm very much aware that there are only six of us here now. Two older men at the high top bar, talking in hushed voices and occasionally laughing so loud that I have to take a peek at them.

And one other couple who are seated at a table in the corner of the bar. The couple who just left had been sitting with them. All four are older than I am. I'd guess married with children and having a night out on the town.

And then there's the bartender and me.

"I'm not really from here, no."

"Just passing through?" he asks me as he walks toward the bar. I'm a table away, but he keeps his eyes on me as he reaches for a glass and hits the tap to fill it with something dark and decadent.

"I'm thinking about going to the university actually. To study business. I came to check it out." I don't tell him that I'm putting down some temporary roots regardless of whether or not I like the school here. Every year or so I move somewhere new … searching for what could feel like home.

His eyebrow raises and he looks me up and down, making me feel naked. "Your ID isn't fake, right?" he asks and then tilts the tall glass in his hand to let the foam slide down the side.

"It isn't fake, I swear," I say with a smile and hold up my hands in defense. "I chose to travel instead of going to college. I've got a little business, but I thought finally learning more about the technicalities of it all would be a step in the right direction." I pause, thinking about how a degree feels more like a distraction than anything else. It's a reason to settle down and stop moving from place to place. It could be the change I need. Something needs to change.

His expression turns curious and I can practically hear all the questions on his lips. *Where did you go? What did you do? Why did you leave your home so young and naïve?* I've heard them all before and I have a prepared list of answers in my head for such questions.

But they're all lies. Pretty little lies.

He cleans off the glass before walking back over and pulling out the seat across from me.

Just as the legs of the chair scrape across the floor, the door behind me opens again, interrupting our conversation and the soft strums of the acoustic guitar playing in the background.

The motion brings a cold breeze with it that sends goosebumps down my shoulder and spine. A chill I can't ignore.

The bartender's ass doesn't even touch the chair. Whoever it is has his full attention.

As I lean down to reach for the cardigan laying on top of my purse, he puts up a finger and mouths, "One second."

The smile on my face is for him, but it falters when I hear the voice behind me.

Everything goes quiet as the door shuts and I listen to them talking. My body tenses and my breath leaves me. Frozen in place, I can't even slip on the cardigan as my blood runs cold.

My heart skips one beat and then another as a

rough laugh rises above the background noise of the small bar.

"Yeah, I'll take an ale, something local," I hear Daniel say before he slips into view. I know it's him. That voice haunted me for years. His strides are confident and strong, just like I remember them. And as he passes me to take a seat by the bar, I can't take my eyes off of him.

He's taller and he looks older, but the slight resemblance to Tyler is still there. As my heart learns its rhythm again, I notice his sharp cheekbones and my gaze drifts to his hard jaw, covered with a five o'clock shadow. I'd always thought of him as tall and handsome, albeit in a dark and brooding way. And that's still true.

He could fool you with his charm, but there's a darkness that never leaves his eyes.

His fingers spear through his hair as he checks out the beer options written in chalk on the board behind the bar. His hair's longer on top than it is on the sides, and I can't help but to imagine what it would feel like to grab on to it. It's a fantasy I've always had.

The timbre in his voice makes my body shudder.

And then heat.

I watch his throat as he talks, I notice the little movements as he pulls out a chair in the corner of the bar across from me. If only he would look my way, he'd see me.

Breathe. Just breathe.

My tongue darts out to lick my lips and I try to avert my eyes, but I can't.

I can't do a damn thing but wait for him to notice me.

I almost whisper the command, *look at me*. I think it so loud I'm sure it can be heard by every soul in this bar.

And finally, as if hearing the silent plea, he looks my way. His knuckles rap the table as he waits for his beer, but they stop mid-motion when his gaze reaches mine.

There's a heat, a spark of recognition. So intense and so raw that my body lights, every nerve ending alive with awareness.

And then it vanishes. Replaced with a bitter chill as he turns away. Casually. As if there was nothing there. As if he doesn't even recognize me.

I used to think it was all in my mind back then. Five years ago when we'd share a glance and that same feeling would ignite within me.

But this just happened. I know it did.

And I know he knows who I am.

With anger beginning to rise, my lips part to say his name, but it's caught in my throat. It smothers the sadness that's rising just as quickly. Slowly my fingers curl, forming a fist until my nails dig into my skin.

I don't stop staring at him, willing him to look at me and at least give me the courtesy of acknowledging me.

I know he can feel my eyes on him. He's stopped

rapping his knuckles on the table and the smile on his face has faded.

Maybe the crushing feeling in my chest is shared by both of us.

Maybe I'm only a reminder to him. A reminder he ran away from too.

I don't know what I expected. I've dreamed of running into Daniel so many nights. Brushing shoulders on the way into a coffee shop. Meeting each other again through new friends. Every time I wound up back home, if you can even call it that, I always checked out every person passing me by, secretly wishing one would be him. Just so I'd have a reason to say his name.

Winding up at the same bar on a lonely Tuesday night hours away from the town we grew up in ... that was one of those daydreams too. But it didn't go like this in my head.

"Daniel." I say his name before I can stop myself. It comes out like a croak and he reluctantly turns his head as the bartender sets down the beer on the wooden table.

I swear it's so quiet, I can hear the foam fizzing as it settles in the glass.

His lips part just slightly, as if he's about to speak. And then he visibly inhales. It's a sharp breath and matches the gaze he gives me. First it's one of confusion, then anger ... and then nothing.

I have to remind my lungs to do their job as I clear my throat to correct myself, but both efforts are in vain.

He looks past me as if it wasn't me who was trying to get his attention.

"Jake," he speaks up, licking his lips and stretching his back. "I actually can't stay," he bellows from his spot to where the bartender, apparently named Jake, is chucking ice into a large glass. The music seems to get louder as the crushing weight of being so obviously dismissed and rejected settles in me.

I'm struck by how cold he is as he gets up. I can't stand to look at him as he readies to leave, but his name leaves me again. This time with bite.

His back stiffens as he shrugs his thin jacket around his shoulders and slowly turns to look at me.

I can feel his eyes on me, commanding me to look back at him and I do. I dare to look him in the eyes and say, "It's good to see you." It's surprising how even the words come out. How I can appear to be so calm when inside I'm burning with both anger and … something else I don't care to admit. What a lie those words are.

I hate how he gets to me. How I never had a choice.

With a hint of a nod, Daniel barely acknowledges me. His smile is tight, practically nonexistent, and then he's gone.

Possessive is Available Now!

SNEAK PEEK OF FORGET ME NOT

I fell in love with a boy a long time ago.

I was only a small girl. Scared and frightened, I was taken from my home and held against my will. His father hurt me, but he protected me and kept me safe as best he could.

Until I left him.

I ran the first chance I got and even though I knew he

wasn't behind me, I didn't stop. The branches lashed out at me, punishing me for leaving him in the hands of a monster.

I've never felt such guilt in my life.

Although I survived, the boy was never found. I prayed for him to be safe. I dreamed he'd be alright and come back to me. Even as a young girl I knew I loved him, but I betrayed him.

Twenty years later, all my wishes came true.

But the boy came back a man. With a grip strong enough to keep me close and a look in his eyes that warned me to never dare leave him again. I was his to keep after all.

Twenty years after leaving one hell, I entered another. Our tale was only just getting started.

It's dark and twisted.

But that doesn't make it any less of what it is.

A love story. Our love story.

PROLOGUE

Robin

I can wait here longer than he can stand to stay away. I know that much.

A small grin pulls at my lips as I pick at the thread on the comforter. Always picking and waiting. There's nothing else to do in this room.

My head lifts at the thought, drawing my eyes to the blinking red light. And he's always watching. The sight of the camera makes my stomach churn, but only for a moment.

The sound of heavy boot steps walking down the stairs outside the closed door makes my heart race. I stare at the doorknob, willing it to turn and bring him to me.

I've waited too long for him.

The sound of the door opening is foreboding. If anyone other than me was waiting for him, I'd assume they'd have terror in their hearts. But I know him. I understand it all. The pain, the guilt. I know firsthand what it's like when the monster is gone and you only have your own thoughts to fight. Your memories and regrets. It's all-consuming.

And there's no one who can understand you. No one you trust, whose words you can believe are genuine and not just disguised pity.

But he knows me, and I know him. Far too well; our pain is shared.

His broad shoulders fill the doorway and his dark eyes meet mine instantly. He barely touches the door and it closes behind him with a loud click that's only a hair softer than my wildly beating heart.

It's hard to swallow, but I do. And I ignore the heat, the quickened breath. I push it all down as he walks toward me, closing the space with one heavy step at a time.

He stops in front of me, but doesn't hesitate to cup my chin in his large hand and I lean into his comforting touch. I know to keep my own hands down though and I grip the comforter instead of him.

It's a violent pain that rips through me, knowing how scarred he is. So much so, that I have to hold back everything. I'm afraid of my words, my touch. He's so close to being broken beyond repair and I only want to save him, but I don't know how.

We're both damaged, but the tortured soul in front of me makes me feel everything. He makes me want to live and heal his tormented soul. But how can I, when I'm the one who broke him by running away?

"My little bird," he whispers and it reminds me of when we were children. When we were trapped together.

He's not the boy who protected me.

He's not the boy whose eyes were filled with a darkness barely tempered with guilt.

He's not the boy I betrayed the moment I had a chance.

He's a man who's taking what he wants.

AND THAT'S ME.

CHAPTER 1

Robin

One week before

"*D*octor Everly?" a soft voice calls out, breaking me from my distant thoughts as another early spring chill whips through my thin jacket and sends goosebumps down my body. I slowly turn my head to Karen. Her cheeks are a little too pink from a combination of the harsh wind and a heavy-handed application of blush, and the tip of her nose is a bright red.

I grip my thin jacket closer, huddling in it as if it can protect me from the brutal weather. It's too damn cold for spring, but I suppose I'd rather be cold and uncomfortable out here. Today especially.

I give Karen a tight smile, although I don't know why. It's not polite to smile out here, or is it? "How are you doing?" I ask her as she walks closer to me.

She nods her head, taking in a breath and looking past me at the pile of freshly upturned dirt. "It hurts still. It's just so sad." Karen's only twenty-three, fresh out of college and new to this. I'm new to it too. Marie was the first patient I've had who killed herself.

Sad isn't the right word for it. Devastating doesn't even begin to describe what it feels like when a young girl in your care decides her life is no longer worth living.

I clear my throat and turn on the grass to face her. The thin heels of my shoes sink into the soft ground, and I have to balance myself carefully just to stand upright.

"It is," I tell Karen, not sure what else to say.

"How do you handle…" her voice drifts off.

I don't know how to answer her. My lips part and I shake my head, but no words come out.

"I'm so sorry, Robin," she says and Karen's voice is strong and genuine. She knows how much Marie meant to me. But it wasn't enough.

I try to give her an appreciative smile, but I can't. Instead, I clear my tight throat and nod once, looking back to where Marie's buried.

"Are you okay?" she asks me cautiously, resting a hand on my arm, trying to comfort me. And I do what I shouldn't. *I lie.*

"I'm okay," I tell her softly, reaching up to squeeze her hand.

As I tuck a loose strand of hair behind my ear, a gust of wind flies by us and a bolt of lightning splits the sky into pieces, followed a few seconds later with the hard crack of thunder.

Karen looks up, and in an instant the light gray clouds darken and cue the storm to set in. It's only the two of us left here and it looks like the weather won't have us here any longer, leaving Marie all alone. I think deep inside that's how she wanted it all along. She didn't want a shrink to give her advice.

Who was I to help her? The guilt washes through me and the back of my eyes prick with unshed tears as I take in a shuddering breath, shoving my hands in my pockets and turning back to her grave.

As much as I'd like to believe I'll let her rest now, I know I'll be back. It's selfish of me. She just wanted to be left alone. She needed that so her past could fade into the background. I know that now; I wish I knew it then.

"She's in a better place," Karen whispers and my gaze whips up to hers. She doesn't have the decency to look me in the eyes and I have to wonder if she just said the words because she thinks they're appropriate. Like it's something meant to be said when talking of the dead, or maybe she really believes it.

Karen turns to walk toward her car as the sprinkling of rain starts to fall onto us. She looks back over her shoulder, waiting for me and I relent, joining her.

I'm sorry, Marie.

As the cold drops of rain turn to sheets and my hair dampens, my pace picks up. It doesn't take long until we're both jogging through the grass and then onto the pavement of the parking lot, our heels clicking and clacking on the pavement with the sound of the rain.

I barely hear her say goodbye and manage a wave behind me as I open my car door and sink into the driver seat.

I just wanted to help Marie. I could see so much of myself in her. We were almost the same age. She had the same look in her eyes. The same helplessness and lack of self-worth. I wanted to save her like my psychiatrist saved me.

But how could I? I'm not over my past. I should have known better. I should have referred her to someone more capable. Someone who had less emotional investment. I pushed too hard. *It's my fault.*

The pattering of rain on the car roof is eerily rhythmic as I dig through my purse, shivering and shoving the wet hair out of my face. The keys jingle as I shove them into the ignition, turning on the car and filling the cabin with the sounds of the radio.

I'm not sure what song's on but I don't care because I'm quick to turn the radio off. To get back to the silence and the peace of the rainfall. I slump in my seat, staring at the temperature gauge. When I look up, I see Karen drive away in the rearview mirror. Watching her car drive out of sight, my eyes travel to my reflection.

I scoff at myself and wipe under my eyes. I look dreadful. My dirty blonde hair's damp and disheveled, my makeup's running. I lift the console and grab a few tissues to clean myself up before sluggishly removing my soaked jacket and tossing it in the backseat. The heater finally kicks on, and I still can't bring myself to leave.

I look back into the mirror and see that I'm somewhat pulled together, but I can't hide the bags under my eyes. I can't force a false sense of contentment onto my face.

I close my eyes and take in another deep breath, filling my lungs and letting it out slowly. I need sleep. I need to eat. It's been almost a week since I found out about Marie. A week of her no longer being here to call and check in on. Tears stream freely down my cheeks. I tried so hard not to cry; I learned a long time ago that crying doesn't help, but being forced to leave her is making me helpless to my emotions.

That first night I almost cried, but instead I resorted to sleeping pills. A wave of nausea churns in my stomach at the thought of what I did. It was so easy to just take one after the other. Each one telling me it'd be over soon. After downing half the bottle, I knew what I was doing. But the entire bottle was too much and it all came back up before I could finish it. Thank God for that. I'm not well, and I'm sure as hell not in a position to help others.

My hand rests against my forehead as I try to calm down, as I try to rid myself of the vision of Marie in my office, but other memories of my past persist there, waiting for this weakness.

I can't linger any longer. Putting the car into reverse, I back out of my spot, turning and seeing Marie's plot in the distance as I back up.

Grief is a process, but guilt is something entirely different. It's becoming harder and harder to separate the two, and I know why.

She reminds me of *him*.

Of a boy, I knew long ago. The turn signal seems louder than ever as I wait at the exit to turn onto the highway. *Click, click, click.*

Each is a second of time that I'm here and they're not. *Click, click, click.*

The cabin warms as I drive away, merging onto the highway.

Maybe all this has nothing to do with Marie.

Maybe it's just the guilt that summons the vision of his light gray eyes from the depths of my memory.

Maybe it's because I'm to blame for both of their deaths.

Forget Me Not is Available Now!

CPSIA information can be obtained
at www.ICGtesting.com
Printed in the USA
BVHW082013200222
629613BV00006B/93